ROBOT RACERS

BOOK 1

Robot Racers is published in the United States by
Stone Arch Books, A Capstone Imprint
1710 Roe Crest Drive
North Mankato, Minnesota 56003
www.capstonepub.com

First published in 2013 by Curious Fox,
an imprint of Capstone Global Library Limited
7 Pilgrim Street, London, EC4V 6LB
Registered company number: 6695582
www.curious-fox.com

Text © Hothouse Fiction Ltd 2013
Series created by Hothouse Fiction
www.hothousefiction.com
The author's moral rights are hereby asserted.

Library of Congress Cataloging-in-Publication Data is available on the Library
of Congress website.

ISBN: 978-1-4342-6570-8 (hardcover)
ISBN: 978-1-4342-7936-1 (paperback)

Summary: Jimmy and his new robot, Maverick, compete in the first leg of the
Robot Races, which takes place in the Grand Canyon.

Artistic Elements: Shutterstock

Designer: Alison Thiele

With special thanks to David Grant.

Printed in the United States of America in Stevens Point, Wisconsin.
022014   008034

ROBOT RACERS
CANYON CHAOS

BY AXEL LEWIS

STONE ARCH BOOKS™
a capstone imprint   www.capstonepub.com

TABLE OF CONTENTS

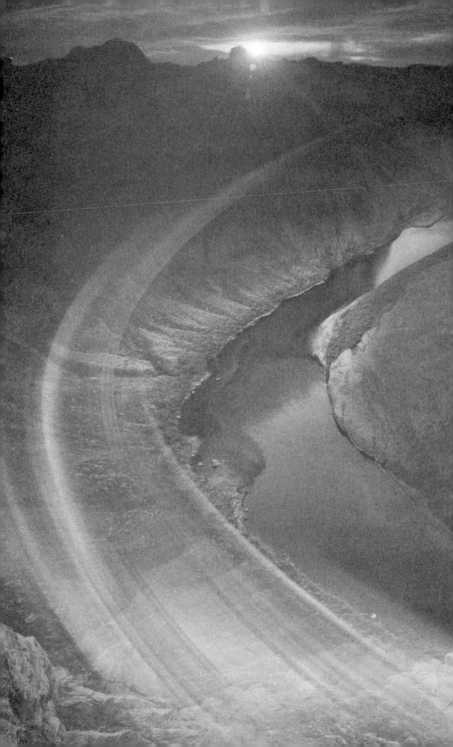

CHAPTER 1
MEET JIMMY

"They're coming up to the finish line!" said Jimmy. "And they're neck and neck! Come on, Big Al! Faster, Crusher, faster!"

Jets of flame shot from Crusher's exhaust. The robot racer pushed forward. Clouds of dust formed as Big Al drove the giant machine into the lead. He was now ahead of Layla Jones and her racer, Aqua.

Layla launched Aqua straight into a shark-infested lake. The robot dove through the water like a torpedo. Big Al yanked on the steering wheel. Crusher swerved to avoid the water, taking a longer route through the forest.

Crusher's rotor blades whirred, hurling trees in the air as he crashed between branches. Big Al turned the wheel sharply to the right. His racer rejoined the track a second in front of Layla.

"Watch out!" cried Jimmy.

Suddenly Professor Plank and his robot, The Gadgetator, were on their tails. The professor threw a perfectly timed smoke grenade. A thick, black cloud smothered all three racers.

When the smoke cleared, The Gadgetator was in the lead. Jimmy held his breath as Big Al fired Crusher's jet engine one last time and pulled alongside The Gadgetator. Professor Plank began to release another smoke grenade, but before he had the chance, out came a sharp rod from a hatch on Crusher's side. It jabbed at The Gadgetator. The robot swerved violently, spinning off the road into a ditch. Crusher roared toward the finish line.

"Did you see that? Did you?" shouted Jimmy.

"Of course I saw it," his friend Max replied. "I'm holding the phone you're watching it on! And we've seen it twice already this morning."

The two boys stood in the school playground, watching a rerun of the final round of the Robot Races Championship. Their faces were glued to the 3D phone screen as their heroes, Big Al and Crusher, sailed over the finish line.

They yelled with joy as Big Al leaped down from his cockpit and punched the air. They clapped as Crusher gently picked Big Al up and swung him around in the air, firing his boosters in triumph.

Every year, millions of people around the world cheered on their favorite driver and robot racer as they competed for the ten-million dollar prize. It was the biggest event in motorsport history. Every boy and girl in the world dreamed of winning the championship trophy.

On the screen, the picture changed and a commercial came on.

"Brand-new from Leadpipe Industries," bellowed a voice. "Crusher toy with rotating crane pincers that REALLY work!"

Jimmy and Max watched as the picture changed to the toy of The Gadgetator.

"Available in four different colors!"

There was even an action figure of Lord Leadpipe, the multi-trillionaire robot genius who had invented the Robot Races. He had bright red cheeks, a long nose, and a monocle.

"I have Crusher, but which one should I get next?" Max asked. "Aqua or The Gadgetator?"

Jimmy sighed. He knew Grandpa would never be able to afford to buy him a robot racer toy.

"I'd love to go to the Robot Races Hall of Fame and see the real robot racers," Max continued.

Jimmy sighed even louder. Grandpa definitely couldn't afford that! Jimmy had lived with his grandpa for as long as could remember. His parents had died when he was a baby. Grandpa had been looking after him ever since.

Living with his grandpa wasn't like being brought up by any normal old person. Wilfred Roberts didn't like watching daytime TV or doing puzzles. He didn't tell Jimmy to wipe his feet or keep his hands off the best china plates.

In fact, Grandpa was more of a big kid than Jimmy. He was always making forts in the yard, building skateboards, and letting Jimmy stay up late. They would make campfires and roast marshmallows as if they were camping.

When Jimmy was at school, Grandpa worked hard driving a taxi. He drove people around all day and sometimes half the night so that he could pay the bills. But no matter how much he worked, they never seemed to have any money.

Jimmy and Grandpa were never hungry. But they ate a lot of ramen noodles. They were never cold. But during the winter they usually put a coat on when they sat down to watch the TV. And when it was really cold, they put on two coats and a hat.

"There are lots of people worse off than us, my boy," Grandpa would say.

Jimmy didn't mind being poor. He wasn't bothered that everyone else in school had a fancy 3D phone. His clunky old phone was held together with sticky tape. It only worked if you tipped your head sideways and shouted, but at least it worked. He didn't care that everyone else in school had the coolest shoes and clothes. He didn't even care that they had plasma walls where they could watch 800 different TV channels and movies. He knew his grandpa was trying his best to make up for the loss of Jimmy's parents, and he loved him for it.

But sometimes Jimmy did wish he could have just one robot racer toy. He knew that if he really wanted one, Grandpa would go without food for a week to pay for it. But he didn't want to ask because if there was one thing that could take the smile off Grandpa's face, it was Robot Races. In fact, Grandpa hated the Robot Races.

Whenever Jimmy switched on the TV to watch them, Grandpa would start muttering to himself. His white fluffy hair would flop and his huge white mustache would sag.

As soon as Lord Leadpipe appeared on the screen to start the race, Grandpa would clench his teeth and start huffing and puffing.

"Lord Leadpipe!" he would say. "He wasn't always a lord, you know. He used to be plain old

Ludwick Leadpipe. But he's always had the same stupid smirk on his face."

"Should I turn it off, Grandpa?" Jimmy would ask.

"Turn off your favorite program?" he'd reply. "I won't make you do that!" And he'd leave the room, muttering as he went.

So whenever he got the chance, Jimmy watched the Robot Races with his friends.

"Let's watch it one more time," he said to Max.

"Again?" said Max. "The bell's going to ring in a minute. And I'm not even supposed to have a phone in school."

"Just the part where Crusher rams The Gadgetator and wins," pleaded Jimmy.

But Max didn't reply.

Instead he was staring at the school gates. Something was heading across the playground. It was getting closer. Closer and louder.

With the roar of an engine and a squeal of brakes, Horace Pelly arrived in a cloud of dust.

"What on earth . . .?" began Max.

"I bet you've never seen one of these before," said Horace with a big grin.

"That's the new Leadpipe F1-X Roboscooter," Jimmy whispered to Max. "They're not even out yet! Not for another year!"

Horace had short, spiky blond hair and a handsome face. He was the kind of boy you'd see on TV selling breakfast cereal or orange juice. His big, pearly white teeth gleamed in the sunlight. He had a permanent tan from the hundreds of vacations he went on with his family. He always had the latest stuff and loved to brag about it.

Horace's dad was a very rich man. He worked with Lord Ludwick Leadpipe at Leadpipe Labs. He was always giving Horace the latest prototype equipment to try out.

Horace had been the first person in school with the Leadpipe Skatotron skateboard. The first one with the Leadpipe Multisport Pop-Up-Super-Stadium. And the only one with the Leadpipe Digital Robocopter. You name it, Horace had it.

Jimmy was used to everyone else having more gadgets than him, but Horace was the worst. He liked to make fun of people like Jimmy because they didn't have the same cool stuff as him.

Once, Jimmy had been walking down the street when it started to rain. Horace and his dad had driven up in their new sports car.

"Jimmy!" Horace had shouted. "Where's your car? I'd call a taxi, if I were you. Oh, yeah, your crummy old car *is* a taxi!" And with that, he and his father had sped off into the distance.

A crowd began to gather around Horace and his new scooter.

"I'd like you all to meet Steve," said Horace.

"Steve?" asked Jimmy.

"That's his name," said Horace, pointing to his scooter. "He's a Special Terrain Endurance Vehicle. Or S-T-E-Ve for short. Say hello, Steve."

"Hello, Horace. What can I do for you?" said a strange voice.

"He can talk?" Jimmy asked. He was totally dumbstruck, which is exactly what Horace wanted. "I thought only the robot racers had personality technology."

"Of course he can talk," said Horace. "And that's not all! Steve? Activate auto-wheelie!" he ordered.

"Right away, Horace," said the motorscooter, revving up his engine. Then he raced off, reared up onto his back wheel, and circled the crowd before returning to Horace. Everyone clapped and cheered.

"He's got all the extras," Horace bragged, pointing to the switches, dials, and screens on the dashboard. "Robonavigation, autopilot, and a homing device if you get lost. And this is my favorite," he said. "Activate fridge, Steve."

"Right away, Horace," the scooter replied and, as if by magic, the dashboard flipped forward.

"The fridge for my lunch. And a few cans of ice-cold Orangiblast. Anyone want one?" Horace looked around.

Jimmy stayed silent as Horace handed out the cans of Orangiblast to his friends.

"Oh, and one more thing," said Horace. "He does this. Steve? Transform!"

With a gentle whirring noise, the scooter split in half, stretched in about six directions at once, and stopped with a quiet clunk. The scooter had turned into an ATV.

The crowd stared, open-mouthed.

Horace smirked. "Dad says when I'm old enough to compete he'll get me a proper robot racer so I can win the Championship. I suppose this will do for now. Who wants a ride?"

Everyone jumped up and down and waved a hand in the air. Everyone except Jimmy.

Horace flicked a switch and started up the engine. It purred and hummed. "Why don't you all get in a line, and I'll take you on a lap of the playground," Horace said, beaming as everyone fought his or her way into a line.

"Except you, Jimmy," he added. "I don't want you on my brand-new F1-X Roboscooter in those gross shoes. You'll make it all dirty."

Jimmy's freckly face went bright red. He wanted to say, "I don't care about having a ride on your stupid scooter." But instead he just scuffed the ground with his foot, making his shoes even dirtier.

Horace revved his engine and hit the gas. He drove straight at Jimmy. "Out of my way, loser!" he shouted as he roared to the other end of the playground. Jimmy had to jump to one side, nearly landing in a huge, muddy puddle.

Horace couldn't get any more annoying if he tried, Jimmy thought.

But he was wrong.

Horace braked sharply and turned in a tight circle. The engine purred powerfully. He looked down at the dark puddle in front of Jimmy and a nasty grin spread across his face. He hunched over his handlebars, revved the engine again, and then accelerated.

Vrroooooommm!

The ATV shot toward Jimmy, the noise of the engine ringing around the playground. At the last second Horace pulled on the handlebars and swerved, skidding into the water. The puddle exploded in a cold, muddy tidal wave, which crashed down on Jimmy's head. Muddy water dripped from his hair, onto his eyebrows, down his nose, and over his chin.

Jimmy closed his eyes and bit his lip. It was difficult to tell if the water in his eyes was tears or puddle water. He wiped it away with a soggy sleeve.

Horace pointed at Jimmy and opened his mouth. Jimmy waited for him to start laughing. But instead Horace's chin dropped and his eyes widened.

Instead of the laugh that Jimmy was expecting, out of Horace's mouth came a scream of terror.

"Aaaaarrggghh!"

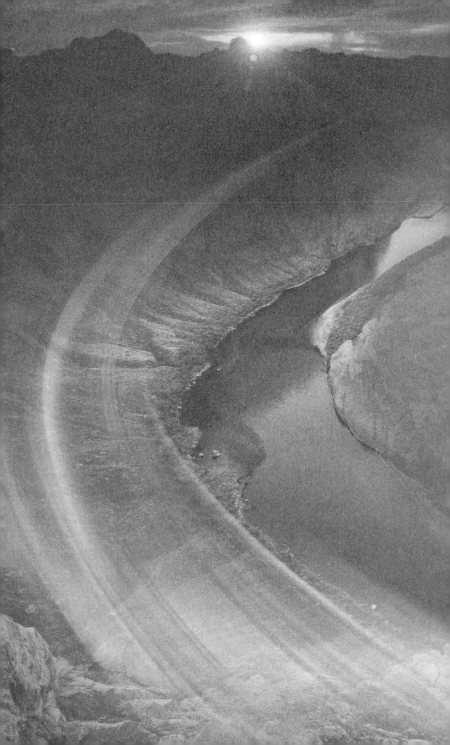

CHAPTER 2
THE ANNOUNCEMENT

"What?" said Jimmy, as Horace yelled. "What is it?"

Jimmy looked around. Everyone else staring, but not at him. They were staring past him. Jimmy turned to look, and his mouth fell open too.

Above them, a huge black shadow was sweeping across the sky. It spread over the school field and across the playground. It was coming straight for them! The sun disappeared. Darkness fell as if the whole town had been swallowed up by a black cloud.

"Aliens," whispered Horace.

Shaking and fumbling, Horace tried to start his roboscooter.

"Start, Steve, start!" he stuttered. But Steve didn't seem to be listening.

All the other kids ran.

"Come on!" yelled Max, as he raced toward the school building.

But Jimmy wasn't scared. He was looking up at the sky and smiling.

Through the darkness he could see the outline of a giant machine. It wasn't an alien craft. It had a huge gold L in a golden ring on the side of it, which could mean only one thing. It was Lord Ludwick Leadpipe's airship.

Jimmy had seen it on TV hundreds of times, hovering above the Robot Races.

"They're dropping something!" squeaked Horace, jumping off Steve. "They're dropping bombs on us!" he shrieked.

Jimmy looked up. Black dots were falling from the airship.

"It's not aliens," said Jimmy, starting to laugh. "It's Lord Leadpipe —"

"They're going to fall on me!" screamed Horace. He threw his hands over his head, ran behind Jimmy and cowered.

"Look!" Jimmy gasped. "They're slowing down!"

He watched in amazement as the black dots seemed to fall in slow motion. One of them floated down in front of him and landed gently on the ground. It looked like a shiny black ball. The little ball started shaking. Then with a pop! it rose up on a pair of robotic legs.

His face frozen in terror, Horace peered over Jimmy's shoulder, watching as the ball started walking toward them. Jimmy couldn't believe how scared Horace was!

"Mmffgllggfff!" said Horace.

"What?" said Jimmy.

"Grsffla inflayunnn!"

"What?" said Jimmy again, staring in amazement as a pair of robot arms popped out of the sides of the little marching ball.

"I said," shrieked Horace, "it's an invasion! We're under attack! Run!"

He kicked his roboscooter out of the way and ran, ducking and darting between the falling robots. But everywhere he ran, the black balls were cracking open and turning into little marching robots: legs first, then arms, then a head, and finally a voice.

"Gather around, everyone," said the little robot in front of Jimmy. "News from Lord Leadpipe."

Horace stopped running and turned around. "L-L-L-Leadpipe?" he stammered.

"Lord Ludwick Leadpipe is proud to announce a new season of Robot Races," the machine continued.

"Wow!" said Jimmy.

"And for the first time ever," it went on, "the Races will be just for children. If you're under the age of sixteen, then you can enter the Robot Races Championship."

With that, the little robot split in half, fired a shower of paper into the air, shrank back into a ball, and rolled away. The great airship thundered into the distance. Pieces of paper fluttered to the ground around Jimmy and Horace.

Jimmy reached out and grabbed one. "Look!" said Jimmy. "It's a leaflet about the new Robot Races!"

He read it out loud, his voice shaking with excitement. "I, Lord Leadpipe, am proud and delighted and honored to announce this special season of Robot Races! A round of qualifying races will be held in every corner of the world, starting just two weeks from today. Only the six very fastest qualifiers will get through to compete in the Championship! So if you've got what it takes to win the most exciting race on Earth, and you're under sixteen years old and have your own robot . . ."

Jimmy's voice came to a halt. Grandpa didn't have enough money for a toy robot racer, let alone a real one. The bubbles of excitement in his stomach all suddenly popped. He was left with a sad, sick feeling in his stomach.

"Gimme that!" said Horace, snatching the leaflet out of Jimmy's hand.

He read it quickly before pulling his phone out of his pocket and hitting a couple of buttons. Then he jammed the sleek device to his ear. "Dad? I need a robot. Lord Leadpipe has just announced . . . Oh, you've heard already. You've done what? Great. Bye."

Horace grinned at Jimmy.

"My dad knows about the Races already. He works for Lord Leadpipe, so he knows everything. And he's already been on the phone with NASA —"

"NASA?" asked Jimmy.

"Yes, NASA," Horace repeated. "The people who build the robo-spaceships. My dad said Leadpipe robots aren't allowed in the competition, so he's ordered NASA to build my robot. I mean, how do you expect me to win the Robot Races Championship if I don't have the very best robo-technology that money can buy?"

"Wow," Jimmy whispered. He could barely even talk.

Horace's grin stretched even further. "What a shame you have absolutely no chance of entering the races. If your grandpa can't afford to buy you a decent pair of shoes, I don't think he'll be ordering a new robot from NASA!"

Horace threw the leaflet in Jimmy's face. "Never mind, Jimmy," he added. "You'll still be able to enjoy watching me on TV, winning the Races. You do have a TV, don't you?"

Jimmy didn't reply. He was watching Lord Leadpipe's airship sail away into the distance. He picked up the leaflet and looked at it one last time. Then he crumpled it into a ball and stuffed it into his pocket.

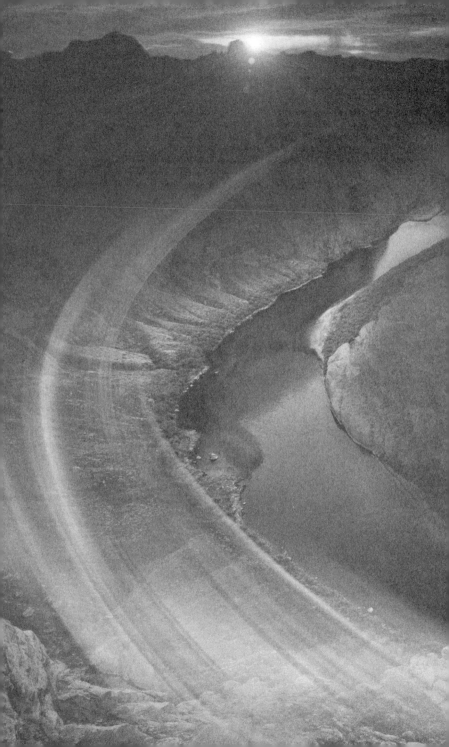

CHAPTER 3
THE PLAN

It was starting to get dark as Jimmy headed for home. He pulled the crumpled leaflet out of his pocket and held it in his hand.

Even the sight of Grandpa's cab parked outside their cozy little house didn't cheer Jimmy up like it usually did. All he saw was the rust on the taxi and the broken garden gate and the front door held together with sticky tape.

Why is Grandpa home from work so early? Jimmy thought as he stepped into the hallway. *I hope he hasn't confused one of his passengers for a celebrity again and invited them home for a cup of tea. That was so awkward.*

Only the other week, Jimmy had arrived home to find a scared-looking young man nervously sipping a cup of tea. It had taken Jimmy half an hour to convince Grandpa that the accountant, who happened to be called Terry, was not the famous actor Leonardo Del Sanchez.

"Oh dear," Grandpa had said. "Well, it was a pleasure to meet you anyway, my friend." And with that, the poor accountant had seen himself out.

"Grandpa! I'm home!" Jimmy called as he walked in. He pulled the leaflet out of his pocket and headed for the kitchen. "Hello!" he called again. Still there was no answer.

Jimmy found Grandpa sitting in the kitchen with his head in his hands, his wild white hair standing on end.

"Grandpa?" said Jimmy quietly.

Grandpa threw his hands down on the kitchen table, looked up, and tried to smile his usual smile. Instead his mustache slowly sagged until its two straggly ends met below his chin.

"What's up?" asked Jimmy. "What's happened?"

"I've had a letter," said Grandpa.

"A letter?" said Jimmy, starting to feel anxious.

"From my boss," said Grandpa. "The head of Total Taxis." Grandpa sighed and began to read it aloud. "Dear Mr. Roberts . . . blah blah blah," he went on, "thank you very much for all your hard work, blah blah blah . . . with great sadness we confirm that your employment with us will end, blah blah blah . . . and we wish you a happy retirement."

Grandpa stared at the letter for a moment, and then his head fell forward and landed on the kitchen table with a thump.

"Retirement?" said Jimmy. "They can't make you retire, can they?"

"They can," said Grandpa, his voice muffled against the tablecloth, "and they have. I gave that company the best years of my life!"

He sighed again, even more heavily this time, and slowly lifted his head off the table. "When

I think of some of the people I've had in the back of that taxi. Did I ever tell you about the time when I picked up Sidney Sharp? He was the world's biggest film star back then. It was just after his big robot movie came out. Did I ever tell you what he said to me?"

"Yes, Grandpa," Jimmy said with a smile. "A few times."

Grandpa's head fell forward again, and his eyes sank shut.

Jimmy couldn't really understand how Grandpa ended up being a taxi driver, or why he loved it so much. As far as Jimmy could see, Grandpa was a genius. He could do math faster than a calculator. He could do two crosswords at the same time — one with each hand — and finish them both in less than sixty seconds.

Last year, the TV had burst into flames just three minutes before the Robot Races final was due to start. Grandpa had put the fire out and had gotten it working again with nothing more than the spring out of an old pen and a paper clip. Jimmy hadn't even missed any of the race.

Grandpa slowly got up and gave Jimmy a comforting pat on the shoulder. "Anyway, how was school? What's that you've got?" he asked, pointing at the paper in Jimmy's hand.

"Nothing," said Jimmy. "It's garbage. I was just going to throw it away."

"Is it your report card?" Grandpa smiled. "Show me," he insisted, holding out his hand.

Jimmy handed it over. He knew what Grandpa would say.

Grandpa took one look at the leaflet and began to shake. "Robot Races?" he cried. "For children?" His face turned red and his mustache twitched. "Leadpipe!" he shouted, thumping a fist on the kitchen table. "That man is making millions and billions every year, but it's still not enough for him!" Grandpa crumpled the leaflet. "If I could get my hands on that man, I'd —"

But suddenly Grandpa stopped. He stared at Jimmy for a long moment. Then a grin spread slowly across his face.

Jimmy knew what that meant. Grandpa was having an idea.

After a long pause Grandpa whispered, "Would you like to be in the Robot Races, Jimmy?"

"No," Jimmy lied, shaking his head. "No way! Why would I want to do that?"

"Because Robot Races is your favorite thing in the world." Grandpa looked at Jimmy searchingly.

"No," said Jimmy. "I like watching them, but that's different. Driving in one of them would be much too —"

"Expensive," finished Grandpa. "You think you'd never be able to race because you'd need your own racer. I'm right, aren't I?"

"No," said Jimmy firmly. "Well, what I mean is . . ." he added quietly, "yes."

And suddenly words started pouring out of his mouth. "Horace Pelly's dad is getting NASA to build him a racer. He gets everything he wants. His dad works for Lord Leadpipe. He gets paid a ton of money. We couldn't afford to buy a racer even when you had a job and now —"

"Buy a racer?" cried Grandpa, standing up. "Buy a racer? Why would we want to buy a racer?" He started bouncing up and down, the ends of his mustache jumping in the air.

Jimmy watched as Grandpa's shaking hands smoothed the Robot Races leaflet flat. Grandpa folded it carefully. Then he grabbed the letter from his boss and crumpled it into a tiny ball. He threw it over his shoulder, and it sailed into the garbage can.

"Follow me," said Grandpa, skipping to the back door, his fluffy white hair streaming behind him. "I've got a surprise," he called over his shoulder. "No!" he said, correcting himself. "I've got a plan!"

CHAPTER 4
GRANDPA'S SHED

Grandpa danced through the yard, skipping between the clumps of weeds and dirt piles. Jimmy followed, anxiously wondering whether Grandpa had gone crazy.

"Where are we going?" asked Jimmy.

"We've arrived," Grandpa announced as they reached the end of the tiny yard. Jimmy looked at the huge bushes in front of them.

"At the bushes?" Jimmy asked.

"At the shed." Grandpa laughed. He reached into the bushes and started pulling them apart. "It's in here somewhere."

Jimmy watched for a second, and then began helping his grandpa clear away the overgrowth. Sure enough, behind the forest was a shed. But not much of a shed. Its wood was rickety and rotting, and it looked like it could be knocked over by a stiff breeze. The only thing about it that looked sturdy was the enormous metal padlock on the rotted wooden door.

"I didn't even know we had a shed!" Jimmy exclaimed.

Grandpa stood on tiptoes and peered through the dirty glass of the shed window.

Jimmy tried to look through the window. "I can't see a thing," he said.

"Good," said Grandpa. "Ready?"

Jimmy watched in silence as Grandpa took off one of his shoes and shook a little gray key into his hand. Grandpa turned the key in the huge padlock.

"Do you always keep that key in your shoe?" Jimmy asked.

Grandpa didn't answer. He was looking left, and right, and behind him, and even up into the sky. Jimmy looked up too, even though he didn't know what he was looking for.

"All clear," said Grandpa, pushing the door open, shoving Jimmy into the darkness of the shed, and shuffling in after him. Grandpa stuck his head back out of the door, gave the garden one last inspection, then pulled the door quietly shut.

Jimmy stood in the darkness. "What's going on, Grandpa?" he asked anxiously, wondering if this was the kind of thing people did when they were having a nervous breakdown.

"Ssshh," said Grandpa. "I just need to find the . . . Aha!"

There was a click, and a blinding light filled the room. Jimmy shielded his eyes, squinting painfully into the brightness.

He opened his mouth to speak. But no sound came out.

Inside the shabby, run-down little garden shed, a wide ramp led down into a large white room that looked like some kind of underground laboratory.

"What . . . what . . . ?" stammered Jimmy as he shuffled down the ramp. "Where am I?"

"You're in my workshop," said Grandpa. "I haven't been here in years."

Around the walls, white countertops were littered with lumps of metal and plastic, with piles of wires tangled up like spaghetti. Rows and rows of tools hung from hooks and, beside them, huge pieces of paper were pinned to the wall: hundreds of drawings of electrical circuits and strange shapes with blades and teeth and wires and labels and all kinds of calculations.

Right in front of Jimmy, there was a desk piled high with rolls of paper, books, folders, a row of neatly sharpened pencils, and a shiny metal hand that looked like the glove from a suit of armor.

With a quick wink, Grandpa clipped two wires to the base of the shiny metal hand on the desk and flicked a switch on a control panel. The hand clenched into a fist.

"Wow!" said Jimmy.

Grandpa wiggled the joystick on the control panel. The fist unclenched and the fingers of the metal hand wiggled too, as though they were scratching an invisible itch.

"That's amazing!" said Jimmy. "How come there's a whole building under the back yard that I didn't know about?"

"When I was younger," explained Grandpa, "I was what they used to call 'a whiz kid.'"

"What do you mean?" asked Jimmy. "What did you do?"

"I invented things," said Grandpa, smiling modestly. "Well, one thing in particular."

"What?" Jimmy stared at Grandpa.

"There it is!" said Grandpa, pointing at the roof.

Jimmy looked up. Grandpa was pointing at something moving across the ceiling. It looked like a cookie tin on tank tracks. When it got to the edge of the ceiling, it slowly drove down the wall and onto the floor, whirring and humming.

"It's still working!" cried Grandpa happily. "No wonder it's so tidy in here!"

"But what is it?" asked Jimmy.

"An old-fashioned robot," said Grandpa. A little door opened in the top of the cookie tin. A mechanical arm reached out. It seemed to be waving at Jimmy.

"A robot?" gasped Jimmy, his mouth hanging open in amazement. "A real one?"

"Yes, but it's pretty basic. Well," said Grandpa with a laugh, "it was the first one ever invented."

"You . . ." began Jimmy. "You invented the world's first robot?"

"Well, yes," said Grandpa. "Yes, I suppose I did."

"Why didn't you tell me?" said Jimmy.

"I'm telling you now," Grandpa said. "Many years ago, before I became a taxi driver, me and a friend of mine worked together. We imagined and invented all kinds of things that we thought the world might want."

"What kinds of things?" asked Jimmy.

"We were working on a highly advanced lie detector," explained Grandpa. "It could tell if you were going to lie before you even opened your mouth."

"Incredible!" said Jimmy.

"But there was a problem," said Grandpa. "My friend and I couldn't agree on the wiring. I thought I was right. He thought he was right."

"Who was right?" asked Jimmy.

"Who knows?" replied Grandpa. "We stopped working together. He went off in a huff. He took our laboratory assistant with him."

"You had an assistant?" asked Jimmy.

"Yes," said Grandpa. "Hector. Anyway," said Grandpa after a moment, "I carried on working on the lie detector. One day a man came to see me. He said he was from a secret department in the secret wing of the Secret Services."

"The Secret Services? You mean, like a spy?" said Jimmy.

"Sort of," said Grandpa. "He was in the technology and gadgets department. He had heard I was good with electronics and computers, and he wanted me to work on a top-secret project."

"The lie detector?" asked Jimmy.

"No," said Grandpa. "A robot."

Jimmy looked down at his feet. The cookie-tin robot was rushing around his shoes, whirring away and cleaning them with a brush on a stick. It was crazy!

"Yes, just like this little guy here," Grandpa continued, grinning down at the robot.

"The Secret Services wanted you to build a cleaning robot? Why?" exclaimed Jimmy in amazement.

"Do you know how much the Secret Services spend on cleaners every year?" asked Grandpa. "My robot would have saved them a fortune! And there were hundreds of other things they wanted robots for too. Things that they said were classified. So they built me this laboratory. They gave me everything I could possibly need."

"The Secret Services built this?" said Jimmy, grinning excitedly. "Unbelievable!"

"I designed this prototype. I took it to show the people at the secret department in the secret wing of the Secret Services. We had a few troubles to begin with, like the time it ripped their carpet to shreds and ate all the chair legs. But with a few minor adjustments, my plans were finished. I was ready to build a new, improved version of this little robot," Grandpa said, patting the cookie-tin robot affectionately on the lid.

"Did you build it?" asked Jimmy.

Grandpa shook his head sadly. "One night," he said, "I was lying in bed when I heard a noise outside. I looked out of the bedroom window, but I couldn't see or hear anything. And in the morning, I came down to the shed and all my plans were gone. Stolen."

"Stolen?" gasped Jimmy.

"A week later," sighed Grandpa, "the man who I had once thought was my friend, the man who I had trusted with some of my greatest ideas, started his own company. He sold the world's first robot. He had stolen my plans and made his own robot. Within a month, he was a millionaire."

"Who was he?" asked Jimmy.

"His name," said Grandpa, "was Ludwick Leadpipe."

Jimmy stared at Grandpa. "You mean your friend," he said at last, "the friend you worked with and invented stuff with was Lord Leadpipe? So that's why you hate him!"

"Yes," said Grandpa. "Can you blame me?"

"I can't believe it," said Jimmy. "I can't believe Lord Leadpipe would do something like that."

"Neither could I." Grandpa sighed. "And that's why I haven't been in this shed for thirty years. I told the Secret Services I was changing my career, and two weeks after the first Leadpipe robot went on sale I got a job with Total Taxis."

"But why give up all this to be a taxi driver?" asked Jimmy.

"You know where you are with a taxi." Grandpa nodded solemnly. "You can rely on a taxi. They always come when you call. And they don't sneak into your shed at night and steal your finest invention."

He stared at the ground and sniffed. When he looked up again, there was a steely glint in his dark eyes.

"So," said Grandpa, "the time has come to make things right. We are entering you in the Robot Races."

"But . . . but . . . but you hate Robot Races, Grandpa," said Jimmy.

"Not anymore!" cried Grandpa, picking up the robot and spinning it around. "This is our big chance! Do you think I want to spend my retirement drinking tea and weeding the garden? Do you think I'm going to let you miss the opportunity to compete in the Robot Races?"

Jimmy stared at Grandpa in amazement. Had the old man gone crazy? "But I don't even have a racer," he mumbled.

"Don't you see?" said Grandpa. "I'm going to build you a racer! When are the qualifying races?"

"In two weeks," replied Jimmy. His insides were jumping up and down with excitement, but the rest of him couldn't move.

"Better get started then," said Grandpa, sharpening a pencil and spreading out a roll of blank paper. "I'll design you the greatest robot racer the world has ever seen!"

CHAPTER 5
GRANDPA GETS BUSY

Jimmy stared into his soggy cereal. He always ate breakfast with Grandpa. But not today. Or yesterday. Or the day before that. In fact, Jimmy hadn't seen Grandpa for days.

He'd spoken to him through the shed door. He'd left cups of tea on the doorstep. He'd stood outside and listened to the banging and clanking as Grandpa worked on his racer. It was the first thing Jimmy heard in the morning and the last thing he heard at night. It couldn't be long before the neighbors started complaining.

Jimmy was thrilled that his grandpa was building him a robot racer. But he was also a

little worried. A little worried that Grandpa
hadn't seen daylight for days. A little worried
that he was going to wake up and find out it
had all been a strange dream. And a lot worried
about driving a robot racer.

The day before, Grandpa's taxi had
disappeared. In the morning it had been parked
outside the house as usual. But that afternoon,
when he'd gotten back from school, the taxi was
gone. He guessed Grandpa had sold it to pay for
the racer.

*What if Grandpa does all this work and spends
all our money building an incredible robot and I turn
out to be a terrible driver?* Jimmy wondered.

It all made him feel a little sick.

* * *

When he got to school that morning, the
first thing Jimmy saw was Horace Pelly in the
yard, talking loudly to his friends.

"The engineers at NASA are working very
hard on my racer," announced Horace. "My dad

told them it's only a week and three days until the qualifying race and it's got to be ready in time. My dad says he doesn't care what it costs as long as it's the best robot racer the world has ever seen. They're putting in all kinds of extras. I've got a rotograbber and jet-thrusters just like Crusher and lots and lots of other amazing gadgets. They're so top secret I'm not allowed to talk about them."

Jimmy wandered past, trying not to look interested.

"Hey, Jimmy," called Horace. "Come over here."

Jimmy froze, his freckly face glowing scarlet as it always did when he was feeling nervous. "Why?" he asked.

"I want to tell you about my robot racer," said Horace.

"I know about your racer," Jimmy said. "I heard you the first time."

"Well!" huffed Horace. "I thought you'd be interested. But I suppose it must be very disappointing for you. I know I'd feel awful if

I was too poor to buy my own robot and enter the race." He chuckled to himself.

Jimmy wanted to say something. He wanted to say, "My grandpa's building my racer. He invented the world's first robot. He would have been a world-famous robotics expert if his friend, Lord Leadpipe, hadn't stolen the idea and made trillions of dollars out of it." But he didn't. He didn't say a word.

"Anyway," said Horace, turning back to the admiring faces gathered around him, "let me tell you a little bit more about my racer. My dad thought it should be green, but I said no, it has to be black. Shiny, metallic black. With chrome trim and leather —"

The bell rang. Jimmy and Horace and everyone else wandered into school, Horace still chattering away about his racer.

"You okay, Jimmy?" said Max as they sat down.

Jimmy nodded. He tried to think of something to say, but he couldn't stop thinking about the qualifying race. Every time he thought about it, his stomach fluttered and his brain did a somersault.

Jimmy tried to concentrate on his math. Up at the front of the class, the teacher was writing out complicated problems on the board. She was saying something about long division and square roots. But all Jimmy could hear was Horace bragging at the next table.

"Do you know there are hundreds of qualifying races?" Horace was saying. "They're taking place in the United Kingdom, France, America, Germany, Japan, and Australia. All over the world, and all at the same time. The six fastest times in the world will be going through to the Robot Races finals. My racer will win the qualifying race here by miles. My father says that no one in the world will be faster than me. They might as well give me my place in the Championship now."

Jimmy let himself daydream about what it would be like to stand on the winner's podium at the qualifier. The crowd chanting his name and screaming for him. The press cameras flashing. The TV interviewers fighting to ask him questions.

"Jimmy," they were shouting, "is it true your grandpa built your racer?"

But before he could answer, the dream was shattered by Horace's annoying voice.

"It's such a shame you can't take part in the qualifier, Jimmy. I mean, obviously you wouldn't win because I'm going to be the winner, but it would be nice for you to participate. Maybe you could get a pair of robot roller skates. Could you afford a pair of those? I might have an old pair I don't need anymore. You're welcome to borrow them." Horace and his friends laughed.

Jimmy bit his lip. *I'd probably have a better chance of finishing on a pair of roller skates than with Grandpa's robot,* he thought glumly.

At break time, he and Max found a quiet corner in an empty classroom so that they could talk about the qualifier.

"I bet my dad would give you a ride," said Max, "if you want to go. You are going, aren't you?"

"I think so," said Jimmy casually. He wanted to tell Max the truth, but he couldn't quite believe it himself. What if he told everyone he was going to enter the qualifier and then he didn't? He'd never hear the end of it. So he decided to keep quiet.

Suddenly, in the distance, he heard a scream. "What was that?" he asked.

Horace was on the other side of the playground, lying next to his scooter and shouting for help. He was surrounded by his friends, all standing around smirking and doing nothing.

Jimmy looked at Max, and the two of them ran over.

Horace was squirming on the floor, holding his leg and whimpering to himself. "I fell off my scooter," he whined, "and I think I broke my leg!"

"I'll go get a teacher," said Max.

"No!" shouted Horace, sitting up suddenly, then sagging down again. "Wait. Before you go, I want to ask you a favor. I'm not going to be able to drive in the qualifier next Saturday with a broken leg. Jimmy, would you be my substitute? Would you drive my brand-new robot racer for me?"

Jimmy stared at Horace in amazement.

"I —" he began, his mind racing. What would Grandpa say? "Really?" he asked. "Do you really mean it?"

"No!" said Horace. "No, of course I don't mean it. Got you, didn't I?"

He ran off, and everyone else rushed after him. Jimmy watched as they raced around the playground, laughing and shouting. Jimmy sighed, stuffed his hands in his pockets, and went off to a quiet corner, the sounds of Horace's laughter following him all the way.

★ ★ ★

A week went by, and still there was no sign of Grandpa or Jimmy's racer. As he made his way down the street toward his school on Friday morning, Jimmy began to wonder if working twenty-four hours a day was healthy for someone Grandpa's age. He was old enough to retire, after all.

"Grandpa, are you okay?" Jimmy had called through the shed door as he put a cup of tea in front of it.

"I'm fine, my boy," had come the cheery reply.

"The qualifying races are on Saturday," Jimmy had said to the shed door. There had been a moment's silence, and then the hammering and the clanking had started again.

As he stepped onto the playground, Jimmy saw Horace and his usual group of friends standing by the main gate.

"NASA delivered my racer last night," Horace announced.

The crowd of admiring faces around him gasped. Even Jimmy wandered over to listen in.

"He's called Zoom because he's so fast," Horace explained. "My dad says he had to pay NASA a fortune to get Zoom ready in time, but he's worth every penny. Who's going to come and watch the qualifying race to see me win? I expect the whole class will be there. Except you, Jimmy. My dad says your grandpa's so old and blind and deaf he's not allowed to drive that old taxi anymore. Will you have to take the bus? Can you afford it?"

Jimmy suddenly felt himself getting very hot. His cheeks flushed, and he clenched his fists. "What if you don't win?" he asked through gritted teeth.

Horace stared at Jimmy for a moment. "Don't you understand?" he said very slowly. "My racer was built by NASA. Even a fool like you should be able to work that out."

Jimmy felt like he was going to explode. He'd never felt this angry, and for once he stood up to Horace. "Your racer," he snapped, "was built by NASA. But it's going to be driven by an idiot."

And before Horace could say another word, Jimmy spun around, stormed out of the school gates, and headed down the street.

★ ★ ★

CANYON CHAOS

Jimmy ran all the way back home, straight through the house, and into the garden. He plopped himself down on the broken old deck chair Grandpa liked to sit in on sunny days. He closed his eyes, fighting back the tears that were threatening to trickle down his face.

"Hello, boy! What are you doing home? School's only just started," asked Grandpa.

Jimmy looked up. Grandpa was standing in the shed doorway, smoke billowing out from behind him, his hair pointing in every direction, and a lopsided grin on his face.

"What's the matter?" asked Grandpa. "You look like you swallowed a rotten fish."

"I didn't swallow one," said Jimmy. "I just go to school with one."

"What are you talking about?" asked Grandpa.

"Horace," Jimmy replied miserably.

"Ah." Grandpa nodded. "Why don't you tell me all about it?"

"He's entering the race too. He goes on and on about winning, and he said stuff and . . ."

"Don't you listen to him!" said Grandpa sternly, pulling Jimmy out of the deck chair and giving him a big hug. "There's only one boy who can win that qualifier. He's the boy who's wiping his nose on my overalls right now."

Jimmy laughed.

"Here," said Grandpa, digging in his back pocket and bringing out a grubby, oil-spattered handkerchief. "Wipe your nose on that."

Jimmy took the rag and gave his nose a snotty blow.

"If we've only got two days until the qualifier, we'd better get a move on!" Grandpa said.

Jimmy froze. "Grandpa, the qualifier's tomorrow," he said softly.

There was a long pause before Grandpa spoke. "The qualifier's tomorrow?"

"Yes," said Jimmy. "Tomorrow. Saturday."

"You mean it's Friday today?" asked Grandpa in astonishment. "What happened to Thursday?"

"Thursday happened yesterday. Remember?" said Jimmy, prickly sweat beginning to gather on his skin. "And today's Friday. Tomorrow's Saturday. Tomorrow is the day of the qualifier."

There was silence for a moment.

"Is there another qualifier next week?" asked Grandpa eventually.

Jimmy stared at Grandpa, then took a quick peek through the shed door. On the floor were piles and piles of metal, wire, and car parts — parts that didn't look like they belonged on any robot racer Jimmy had ever seen.

Grandpa was smiling hopefully at Jimmy.

Jimmy shook his head. "No, Grandpa," he said frantically. "It's 8 a.m. tomorrow or never."

Grandpa narrowed his eyes and pinched his lips together. Then he nodded, walked into the shed, and pulled the door shut.

The clanking and hammering started again, twice as loud and twice as fast.

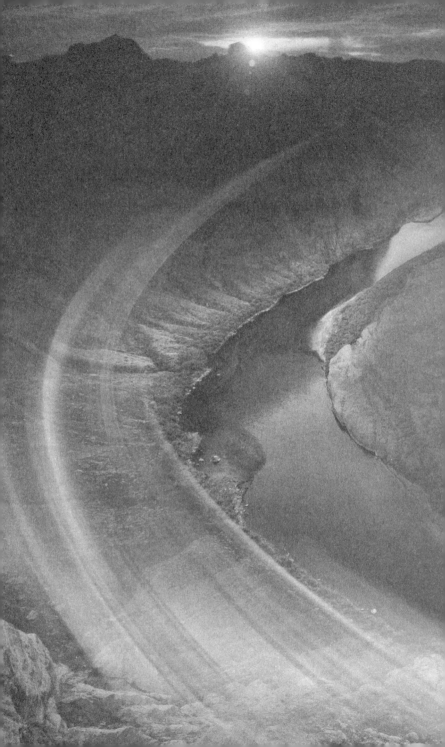

CHAPTER 6
MAVERICK GETS GOING

Jimmy woke up to find Grandpa standing next to his bed. It was barely light outside.

"What time is it?" mumbled Jimmy.

"Six o'clock," said Grandpa cheerily.

"Six o'clock!" grumbled Jimmy. "Six o'clock in the morning? What's going on?"

Grandpa smiled. His eyes were red, his face was pale, and his usually wild white hair sat flat on his head. But his mustache was bobbing up and down excitedly. "Come with me," he whispered.

Still in his pajamas, Jimmy followed Grandpa downstairs, through the kitchen, out to the garden, and over to the shed. With every step, he felt more nervous. He could feel the goose bumps on his arms. A shiver ran down his spine as Grandpa reached for the door handle.

As he stepped through from the natural light of the morning sun to the fluorescent glow of Grandpa's workshop, his vision blurred. But as his eyes grew used to the brightness, he saw a huge, lumpy plastic sheet in the middle of the shed. Something big was underneath it.

"Jimmy," said Grandpa proudly, "I'd like you to meet Maverick." With a flick of his mustache and a flash of his eyes, Grandpa tugged the plastic sheet off Jimmy's new robot racer.

Jimmy stared at it.

"New" wasn't really the right word. For a while, he wasn't sure what he was looking at. It appeared to be Grandpa's taxi, but with dull, gray metal patches welded onto it.

The longer Jimmy stared, the worse it got. The front of the taxi looked like someone had hit it two or three hundred times with a hammer. The roof of the taxi appeared to have things bolted to it. And a tangle of pipes and wires and tubes hung where the back doors used to be.

"What do you think?" asked Grandpa excitedly.

Jimmy tried to think. He looked at the car. He looked at Grandpa. He looked at the car again.

I can't go outside in that! he thought, his heart sinking. *I'll be laughed out of the qualifier when it breaks down right away.*

He thought about sitting next to Horace Pelly at the start line. All the other kids from school would be laughing at him. He turned back to Grandpa, not quite sure what to say.

"I, uh —" Jimmy began.

"Well, don't just stand there," said Grandpa, beaming. "Introduce yourself."

Jimmy looked sideways at Grandpa and wondered what he was talking about. For a second he thought that all those long hours locked away may have made Grandpa imagine things.

"Say hello to Maverick!" Grandpa insisted, pointing at his creation. "He's fully programmed with an intelligence-compiling processor, so the more you talk to him, the more he learns."

"Does it have personality technology?" asked Jimmy nervously.

"Er . . . yes, probably," replied Grandpa, smiling uncertainly. "And Maverick is not an *it*," he added, giving Jimmy a pat on the back. "He's a *he*. So say hello to him."

Jimmy looked at the machine and coughed. "Hello, Maverick," he said quietly.

They waited. Nothing happened. Jimmy's heart sank.

"I don't understand it," said Grandpa, reaching for a screwdriver and chewing the handle thoughtfully. "He should have said hello back. Maybe he will when he's ready."

Jimmy looked disappointedly up and down his racer. He knew he shouldn't feel so let down. He couldn't expect Grandpa to build a racer like the real ones. They just didn't have the money. Grandpa was a genius, but he wasn't a magician.

"Okay!" said Grandpa, clapping his hands and rubbing them together. "It's nearly 7 a.m. The race starts in an hour, which doesn't give us long to get you ready. Come on, Jimmy," said Grandpa, heading out of the shed toward the house.

Jimmy shuffled after him.

"You make breakfast," called Grandpa, "while I find a nice surprise for you."

Jimmy tried to smile. *What kind of surprise could Grandpa have for him next?* he thought.

* * *

Back in the house, Grandpa disappeared into the closet under the stairs. Jimmy put the kettle on and made breakfast. He was beginning to feel sick. His hands were shaking. He had been feeling nervous about the race. And now that he'd seen Maverick, he was terrified. He loved his grandpa, but this wasn't going to work.

What am I going to do? he thought. *I can't tell Grandpa that I don't want to drive that old rust bucket, not after all the hard work he's put in. I'll have to give it a try . . .*

But then Horace Pelly's face crept into his mind again, laughing and making fun of Jimmy in front of everyone.

Grandpa was now deep in the closet under the stairs, muttering to himself. Occasionally something would come flying out: an old Christmas tree, a broom with no bristles, a chair with three legs.

"Aha!" yelled Grandpa. He suddenly appeared in the kitchen doorway, holding a battered crash helmet.

"This was mine when I was seventeen," he said, carefully placing it on the kitchen table. "And now it's yours, Jimmy."

Grandpa patted the crash helmet fondly. A cloud of dust covered the table.

"Thanks, Grandpa," said Jimmy with as much enthusiasm as he could find.

Grandpa placed the helmet ceremoniously on Jimmy's head like he was crowning the next king of the world.

"Come on then, Jimmy," said Grandpa. "Let's go and win that race."

"What about breakfast?" asked Jimmy.

Grandpa looked at the kitchen clock. "No time!" he said. "You can eat any day of the week, but you'll only get one shot at qualifying for the Robot Races. Come on!"

They hurried back to the shed. Grandpa opened Maverick's door and Jimmy climbed in.

There were buttons, switches, levers, and dials covering every inch of the dashboard. Even the doors and roof were covered with them. Jimmy's eyes widened as he looked around. Maverick might look like a scrap heap on the outside, but on the inside it was like being in the cockpit of a robo-rocket.

"How do I —" he began, looking up.

But Grandpa had already climbed onto his rusty old bicycle and was pedaling furiously out of the shed door, heading for the main road.

"I'll see you at the finish line!" he called over his shoulder.

Now what? Jimmy thought.

He glanced back down at the hundreds of buttons, knobs, and levers that lined every inch of Maverick. "But . . . but I don't even know how to make it go!" he said to himself.

"Go?" said an excited electronic voice. "Of course! Why didn't you say so?"

From all around Jimmy came a whirring noise, which grew higher and louder as the racer powered itself up. A red button was flashing right in front of Jimmy.

"Am I supposed to press this?" Jimmy asked nervously, not sure if he should expect an answer from the voice or not. There was no reply. Jimmy shrugged. Then he reached out a finger, took a deep breath, and gently pressed the button.

"Whoopeeeeee!" cried the voice and, with a deafening roar, Maverick lurched forward at an incredible speed, hurling Jimmy back into his seat. He just had time to fasten his seat belt before they crashed through the shed doors, out into the yard, through the neighbor's fence, and onto the road.

They bounced down the road. Jimmy had to turn the steering wheel sharply to avoid hitting the garbage cans belonging to Mrs. Cranky across the street.

"Come on," encouraged Maverick. "Put your foot down. Do you want to be in this race or not?"

For a second, Jimmy's foot hovered over the accelerator pedal as he thought how crazy this all was. He'd never even tried to drive a car before. Now he was at the wheel of a real robot racer!

"Here goes," he said. He pushed his foot to the floor. Maverick's engine roared.

"AAAAAAAAAGGGGHHH!" Jimmy yelled as they tore off down the road.

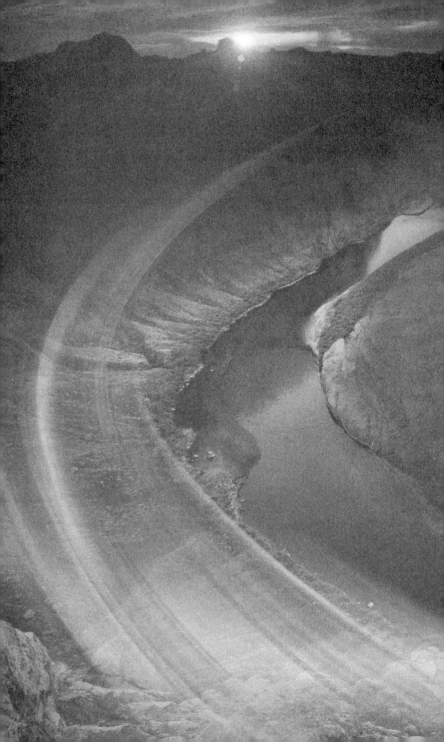

CHAPTER 7
THE QUALIFIER

Jimmy gripped the steering wheel in terror as Maverick sped along. They raced up the street to the top of the big hill. Jimmy could see the rest of the city spread out beneath them.

The roads were lined with safety barriers. Crowds of people were standing behind them, waiting for the race to begin. Even before he saw the crowds, Jimmy could hear them:

". . . nine . . . eight . . . seven . . ." they shouted in time with the huge display board which hovered above the circuit.

Maverick was picking up speed, the houses, cars, and trees becoming a blur as they whizzed past. Jimmy could make out seven other racers, all revving their engines and sending clouds of exhaust fumes billowing into the air. He was relieved to see that three of them looked a little like Maverick: old cars with various pieces of scrap bolted to them.

One of them looked like Jimmy's crash helmet: a dented black fishbowl on wheels. Another one was so tiny Jimmy couldn't see how anyone, even a kid, could fit in it. It was like a big skateboard with something resembling an egg box stuck on top.

And then Jimmy caught sight of a robot racer shaped like a sleek black sports car. The sun glinted off its smooth surface, almost blinding its competitors before the race had even started. And the only thing brighter than the shine from the racer was the big grin on the face of its driver — Horace Pelly. Seeing Horace made Jimmy feel sick.

That must be Zoom, Jimmy thought. *Horace was right. It does look just like a real robot racer.*

". . . six . . . five . . . four . . ."

Maybe I should turn back. This was a stupid idea.

". . . three . . . two . . . one . . ."

"Slow down, slow down," shouted Jimmy. "We're heading for the start line!"

"GO!"

A deafening horn rang out. The spectators cheered.

"Speed up, speed up!" cried Maverick. "They're leaving without us!" He rocketed to the start line, overtaking all the other racers before they could get going.

"We're winning!" shouted Maverick as they sailed ahead.

Jimmy turned to look behind in amazement. Maverick was right. They were in the lead.

"Yes!" shouted Jimmy, punching the air.

But as soon as he'd said it, the whirring of a powerful jet engine could be heard getting louder and louder. A shiny black car pulled up next to him. Jimmy could see the crystal-clear windshield, a glossy chrome steering wheel, and the smiling face of Horace Pelly.

Jimmy watched as Horace's smile disappeared. He was rubbing his eyes in disbelief. He clearly couldn't understand how Jimmy had managed to get a robot racer.

But Horace's shock didn't last for long. He looked Maverick up and down through the gleaming glass of his racer. Then he made a face at Maverick — the same type of face somebody pulls when they notice they've got a big lump of dog poo on their shoe.

Horace shouted something that sounded a lot like, "Ner ner ner ner ner!" Then Zoom's engine roared as he accelerated into the lead.

Two more racers swerved around Maverick, overtaking him with ease. Jimmy had his foot pressed hard on the accelerator, but nothing was happening.

"Oh, no!" Jimmy said. "They're so much faster than us. What can we do, Maverick?"

"Well," said Maverick, "you could change gear for a start."

"How do I do that?" Jimmy asked. "You don't have a gear stick."

"See those paddles flashing on each side of the steering wheel? Pull the one on the right."

Jimmy quickly pulled on the gear paddle. He heard a deep growl coming from the engine. Maverick seemed to flex his mechanical muscles. Then all of a sudden he flew forward. Jimmy hunched himself down over the steering wheel. He focused on the road ahead as they whizzed back past the two racers just in front of them.

"Eat my dust!" Maverick cried as they left them in their wake. "You see, Jimmy. We're going to win this race. Now, show me what you've got."

They entered a tricky section of the course with sharp bends and tight corners. But with Maverick handling the braking and Jimmy controlling the wheel, they flew forward, their tires screeching and the wind whipping at the windshield as they weaved left and right.

"We're doing really well," Jimmy said. "We've left the others behind."

"Of course we have," Maverick replied. "We're robot racers, and that's what we do!"

In the distance they could make out the
cloud of dust that billowed into the air behind
Zoom's jet engine.

"We've got to catch Horace and Zoom," said
Jimmy. "What should we do?"

"See the small red button with the picture of
the flame on it?" Maverick replied. "It's flashing.
Push it."

"What does it do?" asked Jimmy.

"You'll see," replied Maverick.

Jimmy pressed the small red button. For a
moment nothing happened. And then the world
seemed to explode. Jimmy was pinned back
against his seat. Maverick accelerated so fast that
his front wheels left the ground. Before he knew
it, Jimmy was whooping with excitement. He
was really doing it! He was really a robot racer!

At school, he was just a shy, quiet boy.
But out here he could see hundreds of people
cheering for him. He could feel confidence
building, causing his fingers and toes to tingle.
He wasn't scared. He wasn't being laughed at.
And he was in second place!

"Wow!" he cried. "We could actually win this, Maverick!"

"Of course we can," said the robot. "We're gaining on them. They're —" Maverick paused, checked, recomputed. "Yes," he said. "They're slowing down!"

"Why would they do that?" Jimmy asked. But before Maverick could reply, the answer became obvious. Horace had begun to show off.

Zoom's roof was folding away and disappearing. Zoom was going open-top! Jimmy could see Horace sitting casually in the driver's seat with one hand on the steering wheel. The other hand was waving at the crowd and a group of TV cameras that had gathered. A moment later, Horace was standing up and steering with one foot. The crowd was going wild.

Then Horace turned around and saw Jimmy. "I won this race already, Jimmy Roberts. You haven't got a chance," he shouted above the roar of the engines. He dropped back down into his seat and twiddled a couple of knobs on the dashboard.

The motor on Zoom's roof whirred loudly, but nothing happened. Horace punched three more buttons, and the whirring started again, followed by a loud clunking sound.

"No!" screamed Horace over the noise of the wind. "We can't reach top speed with the roof down! Zoom, do something."

"System malfunction," the robot replied. "Roof pod not responding. Unable to override."

"Noooo!" Horace yelled again.

"This is our chance, Maverick," Jimmy said excitedly. "Let's get them."

The race was on!

Zoom slowed to round a curve in the road. Jimmy swerved Maverick wide. He tried to fit through a gap between Zoom and the crash barriers, but he could see Horace gritting his teeth and moving across to squeeze him out of room.

"We're going to hit them!" yelped Jimmy.

"No, we won't," Maverick shouted back. "Watch this." And before he knew what was happening, Jimmy felt the whole world tip sideways. Maverick had thrown himself onto two wheels.

"Go, Maverick, go!" Jimmy cheered. They inched past Zoom and took the lead. Jimmy could see Horace thumping the steering wheel and shouting as they flew past.

Ahead of them stretched a long, straight road. At the end of it, a huge crowd was cheering the two leaders on. They could just make out a man standing with a checkered flag.

"Look!" cried Jimmy. "The finish line! Come on, Maverick!"

"Hold on," Maverick replied, and then he threw himself back onto four wheels.

Jimmy's heart was racing. But Zoom and Horace hadn't given up yet, and Jimmy could see them in his mirrors, dodging and weaving behind them. The jet engine whirred louder than ever, and Zoom inched alongside them.

And in front.

Then Maverick took the lead by a whisker.

Zoom edged back ahead.

They were neck and neck.

The finish line raced toward them. Jimmy's foot was flat to the floor, his grip on the steering wheel steady and solid, his eyes fixed on the checkered flag straight ahead.

"Go! Go! Go!" Jimmy shouted.

"Faster, you useless heap of space junk!" Horace shrieked above the noise.

"This is gonna be tight," Maverick said.

With a *whoosh!* they hurtled past the checkered flag as the crowd screamed their appreciation.

"Did we win? Did we win?" asked Jimmy.

But before Maverick could answer, a huge crowd of people surrounded them, cheering and screaming and chanting.

"We won! We won!" yelled Maverick, his lights and sensors flashing madly as he slowed to a stop in front of the grandstand.

Photographers and TV cameras pushed their way through the crowd. Reporters shouted questions. Even louder than the crowd, a voice echoed from the loudspeakers: "Let's hear it for our winners . . . Jimmy Roberts and Maverick!"

The crowd went wild.

I don't believe it, Jimmy thought to himself. *We won a Robot Race!*

Head spinning and feet stumbling, he climbed out of Maverick's cockpit and into the crowd. From the corner of one eye, he saw Horace get out of Zoom, slam the door, kick it, and stomp off into the distance.

Jimmy could just hear him shouting, "Dad! Dad! Get over here! I want that result changed right now. He cheated! It's not fair. He broke my roof, I know he did. Do something! This is not fair! Not fair at all!"

Just then two figures pushed their way through the crowd toward Jimmy. It was Grandpa and Max.

When Grandpa reached Jimmy, he seemed to be lost for words. But he had a grin on his face that was so big it nearly split his face.

"We did it, Grandpa!" said Jimmy. "We won! We really won!"

"*You* did it, my boy," corrected Grandpa, crushing Jimmy in a huge hug. "You did it."

"Jimmy . . . how did you . . .? Why didn't you . . .? When did you get a robot racer?" asked Max.

"Didn't I tell you my grandpa was an inventor?" replied Jimmy, trying to look cool. But he couldn't help the grin that spread across his face as Max high-fived him.

"You were awesome," Max said. "I've never seen a race like it! And I've seen every Robot Race in history!"

Just then, the crowd surged around them. Before Jimmy could say anything else to his grandpa or best friend, he was being carried away. He was swept toward a podium where a camera was pointing right at him. Behind the camera was a huge video screen.

"Ladies and gentlemen," boomed a voice from the loudspeakers. "Please wait as we calculate the results of the qualifiers from all around the world."

The video screen flickered. Numbers and names flashed up, whizzing by and whirring, as the results from the hundreds of qualifiers were beamed in. Jimmy held his breath. He had won his qualifier, but surely he wouldn't be one of the fastest racers in the world, would he?

"Remember," echoed the voice, "only the six fastest qualifiers will win a place in the Robot Races Championship. And the results are in!"

The screen went blank for a moment. Then it flickered, and an image appeared. It was the round, red face of Lord Ludwick Leadpipe. His monocle gleamed as a beady black eye peered through it.

"The results of the qualifiers are as follows," announced Lord Leadpipe. He paused and checked his notes, cleared his throat, scratched his ear, and cleared his throat again. The crowd was absolutely silent, leaning forward in their seats as they waited.

"With the fastest qualifying time in the world, in first place," said Lord Leadpipe, "from the United States of America, Chip Travers and his racer, Dug."

Lord Leadpipe's face disappeared. In its place appeared the face of an African-American boy in a baseball cap, whooping and screaming. He was on top of a huge yellow and gold robot shaped like a digger. The crowd cheered.

"In second place," announced Lord Leadpipe, "from Japan, Princess Kako and her racer, Lightning."

The face of the bouncing boy in the baseball cap vanished. A solemn Japanese girl appeared, leaning against a motorbike racer. Princess Kako smiled. She nodded gently at the camera as she received her round of applause.

"In third place," said Lord Leadpipe, "from Australia, Missy McGovern and her racer, Monster."

A red-haired girl filled the screen. She was seated comfortably on the giant wheel of her monster truck racer. She gave a big thumbs-up to the camera.

"In fourth place," said Lord Leadpipe, "from Egypt, Samir Bahur and his racer, Maximus."

A serious-looking boy appeared on the giant screen. The boy was scowling at the camera. It was hard to believe he'd just won the race of his life. Behind him was an impressive hovercraft racer with giant fan engines that looked like they'd been taken straight from a windmill.

"In fifth place," said Lord Leadpipe, "from Sweden, Olaf Trygvasson and his racer, Velocitron."

The screen showed a stocky figure in a leather jacket, his head covered in a huge black crash helmet. He waved at the camera.

"And finally, in sixth place, from the United Kingdom —"

The crowd fell silent.

"Jimmy Roberts and his racer, Maverick," announced Lord Leadpipe.

Jimmy was stunned. There on the screen was a pale, skinny blond boy with freckles all over his face.

It's me! Jimmy thought.

From somewhere in the background he could hear Lord Leadpipe continuing, "And that's the end of the qualifying rounds. Thank you all for watching, racing fans. Tune in next time to see how our six contestants do during the first round of this special edition of the Robot Races Championship." And with a wink to the camera through his monocle, the cheery face of Lord Leadpipe disappeared.

"Woo-hoo!" yelled Grandpa.

"You did it!" cheered Max.

I must be dreaming, Jimmy thought. *I can't really have qualified for the Robot Races Championship, can I?*

CHAPTER 8
THE COMPETITION

The next day, at exactly 8:57 a.m., Jimmy and Grandpa made their way outside. The sky above them darkened. Lord Leadpipe's giant airship floated overhead, blocking out most of the sun. It looked like it was still night.

Maverick drove out of the shed. "How do I look, Jimmy?" he asked.

Jimmy squinted at his racer. Grandpa had smartened up Maverick's appearance. He looked more like a professional robot racer, but there were still gray patches and lumps and bumps. Maverick wouldn't be winning a beauty contest anytime soon.

"You look amazing," said Jimmy, hoping that he sounded convincing.

Jimmy and Grandpa packed a suitcase of clothes and Grandpa's tool bag safely into Maverick's trunk before climbing into the front seats. Jimmy looked around Maverick's cockpit. There were even more buttons and levers and switches than he remembered.

Grandpa had spent half the night working on Maverick, making modifications. He kept saying, "Things are only going to get tougher from here on out, my boy. I want Maverick to be prepared for any situation. Who knows what Leadpipe will have planned for you?"

Before Jimmy could investigate the dials and knobs any further, there was a *boom!* that shook the earth. A huge platform was lowered from the airship on thick metal chains.

"Amazing!" said Jimmy.

"Incredible!" Maverick added.

"Show-off," Grandpa muttered.

The platform reached the ground. Jimmy drove Maverick onto it.

Grinding and creaking, the chains were pulled up again. Jimmy peered over the edge of the platform as they rose higher and higher into the sky. The platform climbed above the trees, above the tops of the houses, and kept on going until it was high into the clouds.

Grandpa had his eyes squeezed shut. His skin had turned a nasty green color, as though he might throw up at any moment. But for Jimmy, this was one of the most exciting moments of his life.

I can't wait to tell Max about this. I'm actually going to get to see inside Lord Leadpipe's private airship! he thought.

Finally they heard a loud clunk. Jimmy looked around at his new surroundings in amazement. Everywhere Jimmy looked, people were rushing around carrying equipment or shouting orders. There were electronic signs pointing to places like the swimming pool, movie theater, and restaurants.

And the room they had been lifted into was actually the most enormous workshop Jimmy had ever seen. Under brilliant white spotlights, the mechanics and pit crews for each of the racers worked on their robots. None of them even noticed Jimmy, Grandpa, and Maverick make their entrance.

As they opened Maverick's doors and climbed out, Jimmy saw that the platform had lifted them directly into their own work station. It had shelves, cabinets, and tool chests full of state-of-the-art gadgetry. It made Grandpa's battered old tool kit look prehistoric.

But before he could say a word, Jimmy felt a tap on his shoulder. He spun around to see a tall man with huge eyebrows grinning at him. The man wore a dark blazer with a gold L for Leadpipe on the breast pocket. A huge red scarf was tucked under his chin, and two balls of cotton were poking out of his ears. Jimmy guessed this was to help block out the noise from all the engines.

"Joshua Johnson," said the tall man in a loud voice. "Robot Coordinator. I'm in charge of looking after the teams during the competition.

If you have any problems, you see me, okay?"
He grinned at Jimmy and Grandpa.

"And you must be . . ." Joshua Johnson
pulled a clipboard from somewhere behind his
back and stared at it for a moment. "Jimmy
Roberts. Delighted!"

"This is my grandfather," said Jimmy,
nodding at Grandpa. Joshua Johnson moved
along to Grandpa and held out his hand.

"Joshua Johnson, Robot Coordinator," said
Joshua Johnson again. Grandpa shook his hand
and grinned.

"And this must be —" said Joshua Johnson,
peering over Grandpa's shoulder at Maverick.
"Oh," he said. He checked his clipboard again
and squinted at Maverick like he couldn't quite
believe his eyes.

"Is he okay? I mean, has he had an accident?
Will he be able to race?"

Jimmy felt his face going red. "Maverick's
fine," he said quietly.

"I'm more than fine," Maverick chipped
in. "I'm great. Just wait until you see me race,

Bushy-brows. I'll show the rest of these robots a thing or two. You know what they say — looks can be deceiving."

Joshua Johnson looked a little flustered. "Right, right," he stuttered, trying to look as dignified as possible as he wiped a bunch of sweat off his face with a fancy handkerchief. "Come and meet the other racers."

He marched off toward a pit station. A group of ten or fifteen people stood around, all dressed in black baseball hats, black pants, and black shirts. Each shirt had a streak of silver lightning zigzagging down the back.

"Excuse me, excuse me," said Joshua Johnson, edging his way through the mechanics. Jimmy and Grandpa followed him.

The crowd suddenly parted. There, at its center, was a skinny Japanese girl in a silver motorcycle outfit. She stared at them with a serious look.

"Your Highness, may I introduce Jimmy Roberts and his grandfather?" said Joshua Johnson, bowing his head politely.

"Your Highness?" echoed Jimmy in surprise.

"Yes," said Joshua Johnson. "This is Her Imperial Highness, Princess Kako of Japan."

The girl bowed her head. Jimmy did the same even thought he didn't really know what was happening.

"And this is Lightning," the Robot Coordinator said, waving a hand at a large, powerful motorbike with a silver lightning bolt painted on the fuel tank.

Jimmy had never seen a motorbike like it. Lightning had spoilers and exhausts sprouting from every part of his body. His huge, shiny engine looked like it could have been used to power a jumbo jet.

Lightning flashed his headlight in acknowledgement, stretching the tip of one of his spoilers and flexing a pair of turbo jets positioned on each side of the back wheel. He reminded Jimmy of a panther, stretching after a short nap.

Joshua hurried Jimmy and Grandpa along to the next station, where there was even more noise and activity than at the last. Jimmy couldn't believe how intense this entire race was, and it hadn't even started yet!

"This," said the Coordinator, bowing and backing away, "is Missy McGovern and her racer, Monster, from Australia."

Joshua Johnson led Jimmy and Grandpa to a huge monster truck where a short, stocky girl in oil-stained overalls was standing with her hands on her hips.

"What's the point of having self-regulating tire pressure if I have to check it all the time, you useless lump?" she was shouting.

"Gives you something to do," said a metallic female voice from the tiny cab perched on top of the enormous body. "Keeps you from getting bored," it added.

Jimmy had seen pictures of monster trucks before, but standing up close to one for the first time made him realize just how enormous they were. Monster was at least four times as high as Maverick and three times as wide. He was the biggest machine Jimmy had ever seen.

It was impossible to see what kind of gadgetry Monster had from down at floor level, but Jimmy knew that the mammoth wheels alone could crush most of the competition.

"Maybe I'll send you to the dump and get a decent racer," continued Missy, kicking a huge tire affectionately.

"That hurt!" said the metallic voice.

"Good," said Missy, stomping off toward her engineers, who all wore matching oil-stained overalls.

Joshua Johnson grinned with embarrassment. "I'm sure she'll say hello later," he said, "when she's calmed down a little. And this," he went on, hurrying away, "is our next competitor."

He led Jimmy and Grandpa over to a boy of average height with short black hair. His face looked like it had been carved in stone.

"This is Samir Bahur and his racer, Maximus," said Joshua Johnson. "Samir, this is Jimmy Roberts from the United Kingdom."

Samir stared with his cold gray eyes and gave Jimmy a short, sharp nod of his head. "I prefer

to be known as Sammy," he said with a thick
North African accent.

Then, without another word, he turned away
to Maximus, a futuristic hovercraft powered by
two hoverblades. His mechanics were scurrying
around in khaki overalls, checking every inch of
the robot for problems. Barking orders at them
was a broad-shouldered man with a thick black
beard whom Jimmy vaguely recognized, but he
wasn't sure why.

"That's Samir's father, Omar Bahur,"
whispered Joshua Johnson quietly. "He's a
former Robot Races champion himself, and by
far the scariest man I've ever met," he added
even more quietly before hurrying away.

That's where I know him from, Jimmy thought
to himself. *I've seen old videos on Max's phone of
Omar winning races.*

"There is one more competitor we'll be
picking up on the way to the Grand Canyon,"
explained Joshua Johnson over his shoulder as
they walked. "And one other competitor for you
to meet now. He's from the UK too."

Jimmy and Grandpa followed Joshua Johnson toward a sleek, black shiny robocar that looked familiar. Beside it, facing the other way, was a short, skinny boy with a big head. He was dressed all in shiny black leather. The boy turned around and sneered.

Jimmy stared in horror.

"Jimmy, this is —" said Joshua Johnson.

"Horace Pelly," Jimmy gasped.

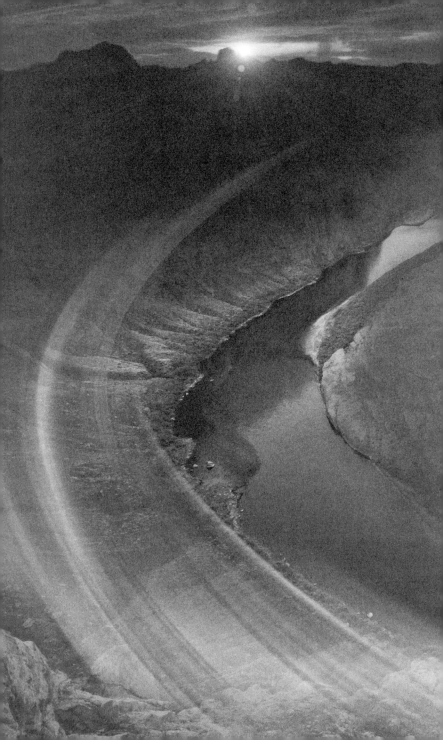

CHAPTER 9
THE RETURN OF HORACE PELLY

"I wondered when you'd finally show up," sneered Horace.

Jimmy said nothing.

"Pleased to see me?" said Horace.

Still, Jimmy said nothing. His mouth seemed to have stopped working.

"These NASA people," said Horace, nodding over his shoulder at a small group of men and women in blue overalls and hats, "are amazing. They've worked wonders with Zoom since the qualifier. He's faster, smarter, and better equipped. He's got thirty-two more features than —"

"But —" Jimmy started.

"Why am I here?" asked Horace, his mouth breaking into that sneer again.

Jimmy nodded.

"That Swedish boy? Olaf something?" said Horace. "Turns out he wasn't a *boy* at all. He was twenty-one years old, so he was disqualified. And I was the next fastest qualifier. So I suppose you could say —"

"Horace!" called a voice.

A tall, slim man marched up to them. He looked just like Horace, apart from the fact that his thick hair was jet black while his son's hair was blond. He had a long, thin mustache which sat just above his top lip. His hair was slicked back. He wore an expensive-looking suit.

"Yes, Dad?" said Horace.

"Stop jabbering at this boy, Horace," said Mr. Pelly, twiddling his mustache irritably between his finger and thumb. "Come with me. We must prepare for victory."

"But you're paying those NASA people to do that for us, aren't you?" whined Horace.

"Not winning the race," laughed his father. "I mean your victory speech. When you're on the winner's podium, you must thank everyone who made your victory possible — especially your beloved father. Oh, and you should probably say something about your mom too, I suppose. Come along and we'll practice it."

And with that, Horace and his father marched off to a silver motorhome parked behind Zoom. The door slid open automatically, and the Pellys disappeared inside.

"Disqualified!" exploded Grandpa. "There's something funny going on here."

"What do you mean?" asked Jimmy.

"I mean," said Grandpa, "that his father has paid someone a lot of money to get him in this race. It's probably something to do with that no-good, cheating snake, Ludwick Leadpipe —"

"Ssshhh!" hissed Jimmy. "Lord Leadpipe's probably on the airship. He'll hear you!"

But there was no need for Grandpa to hush. A voice boomed out of the loudspeakers above their heads and silenced everyone.

"Ladies and gentlemen," it announced, "we have one more competitor joining us, and then we'll be landing at the Grand Canyon racetrack within one hour."

Everyone cheered.

"Well," said Grandpa, "that was quick! Six thousand miles at hyperspeed, and not a whisper of turbulence!"

"Are you impressed with Lord Leadpipe's airship?" asked Jimmy.

"No," replied Grandpa quickly.

Jimmy smiled.

A few seconds later, there was a terrific grinding and whirring noise. The platform on which Maverick and Jimmy had been lifted up to the airship was lowered down to the ground again.

It soon returned with the huge yellow digger that Jimmy had seen on TV just a couple of days before. Five or six mechanics in yellow overalls were now perched on the beefy caterpillar tracks Dug used instead of normal wheels. A boy waved cheerfully from the driver's cab.

"Hi! You're Jimmy!" he yelled in a loud Southern accent. "I saw your picture in the papers. I'm Chip Travers. How are you?"

"Fine, thank you!" replied Jimmy cheerfully.

"This here's my dad," called Chip, pointing at the man sitting next to him. "And this," said Chip, patting the digger's dashboard, "is Dug. Say hi to Jimmy, Dug!"

Dug swiveled his digging arm around to Jimmy. He jumped backward as it swung at him.

Chip laughed. "He don't bite!" he called.

Jimmy edged forward and held out his hand. Ever so gently, Dug grabbed Jimmy's hand in his giant arm and shook it up and down.

★ ★ ★

Jimmy felt like he was in a daze. Just twenty-four hours before, he'd been a nobody. Now he'd done interviews with newspaper reporters, signed autographs, and stood for millions of photos. Plus he was on Lord Leadpipe's airship with the best robot racers in the world.

Jimmy looked over at Grandpa, who was making a few last-minute improvements to Maverick. "Okay. All of the rocket-boosters are supercharged and tightened." Grandpa grinned. "Now, what's next?"

Just at that moment, a voice chimed in over the loudspeaker.

"Ladies and gentlemen, if you move to the viewing area, you will see the Grand Canyon and the race circuit where we will soon be landing."

There was a rush to the row of windows on the far side of the airship. Jimmy and Grandpa managed to squeeze in between Chip Travers's dad and one of Sammy's mechanics. They could see the Grand Canyon and the new racetrack that had been created. They all gasped.

"I've been to the Grand Canyon more times than I can remember," said Chip's dad, "but I've never seen it from up here. Wow!"

Looking down from the airship, the Canyon was like a huge crack in the dusty red desert. There were no smooth roads to drive on. There were just sheer cliffs, solid rock walls, steep hills, and slippery slopes.

Everyone aboard the airship stared in silence as the ground came closer. The Canyon grew larger in the window.

A few minutes later, Jimmy, Grandpa, Maverick, and all the others were safely on the ground. As they made their way to the start line, they could see thousands of fans making their way up to the grandstands. They scrambled over the Grand Canyon, all dressed in brightly colored clothes. Some were carrying banners and flags. Jimmy's heart skipped a beat as he thought of all the people who would be cheering him on both here and back at home.

Camerabots and safetybots hovered above them, darting among the display boards that floated over the racetrack. Some of the boards were counting down the last few minutes to the start of the race. Others showed a video of the racecourse layout. An announcer was explaining the different challenges that the drivers would face, but Jimmy couldn't understand a word that was being said. His mind had gone fuzzy. He looked along the line of racers and suddenly felt very cold and very sweaty.

Come on, Jimmy. Pull yourself together, he told himself.

Once the racers were in line, the mechanics looked over their vehicles to perform final checks. The competitors prepared themselves for the race. Horace Pelly came over, sneering his usual sneer. He was dressed in a custom-made white racing outfit with a red stripe down the arms and legs.

Jimmy looked down at his own racing outfit: jeans, a T-shirt, and an old helmet. He swallowed hard.

"I see you're admiring my outfit," said Horace. "My dad had it invented specially. It's lightweight, titanium, fireproof, and crash proof. My dad says I'm too precious to risk anything less. You're racing in those jeans and T-shirt, I guess?"

"Well, I'm not planning on crashing or catching fire," muttered Jimmy. He hated how

Horace always made him feel. He might have beaten him in the qualifiers, but Horace still treated him like a joke.

"And what modifications have you made to . . . to . . ."

"Maverick?" said Jimmy.

"Yes, that old rust bucket of yours," said Horace. "It's a tough terrain here. I hope you've prepared him for it. My NASA engineers —"

Jimmy turned away and tried to stop listening, but he couldn't help noticing that all of the other drivers were wearing custom-made racing outfits too. Jimmy looked like he was going to play video games.

"Anyway," said Horace, interrupting Jimmy's thoughts, "I've wasted enough time talking to you. I must go and be interviewed by the press." Horace strode over to a group of reporters. Cameras started flashing as he posed and grinned.

Jimmy climbed into Maverick's driver's seat and strapped himself in. Then he looked nervously at the robot racers around him.

Zoom's black paint work shone in the sunshine.

Dug reached out his huge hydraulic arm to high-five people in the crowd.

Towering above the others, Monster was blowing exhaust fumes high into the air.

Maximus the hoverbot revved his fan engines menacingly.

And right next to Jimmy and Maverick, Princess Kako sat aboard her robocycle, Lightning, practicing some moves. Lightning transformed at top speed from motorbike to roborocket and back to motorbike again.

Jimmy noticed that all of the other racers had the names of sponsors splashed across their sides. Zoom and Horace were supported by Gleam Toothpaste — "For a Winning Smile!" Lightning had the words "Tokyo.Pro.Robo. Co. — by Royal Appointment" printed on his mudguards. Chip and Dug were sponsored by Luke's Lasers — "the Brightest and Best." The words "Cairo Construction" were splashed on the roof of Maximus. Missy and Monster

sported the title Robotron Rocket Boots —
"Footwear that Flies!"

Grandpa had called Total Taxis to see if they
wanted to sponsor Maverick. They had said they
would think about it and call Grandpa back, but
they hadn't called.

What am I doing here? Jimmy thought. *I don't
have a chance of winning this race.*

"You all right, my boy?" said Grandpa,
appearing from underneath Maverick, where he
had been making some final adjustments.

Jimmy stared sadly at the other racers.

"You all right, Jimmy?" repeated Grandpa,
louder this time.

"Yeah, fine," Jimmy replied quietly.

"They might look better than Maverick,"
said Grandpa softly, "but they haven't got you
at the wheel, my boy. Don't tell him I said this,"
Grandpa whispered, "but I know Maverick's not
the best-looking racer."

"I heard that," Maverick said.

"But looks aren't everything, though,"
Grandpa continued, grinning so much that his

mustache wobbled. "You wait till you're out there on the track. You'll see."

Jimmy nodded. He hoped Grandpa was right.

"Right!" said Grandpa as he patted Maverick. "I'm off to the first pit stop to get myself ready. I'll see you there!"

Jimmy watched Grandpa disappear into the crowd.

"Racers!" boomed a voice from the loudspeakers. "Take your positions!"

CHAPTER 10
AND THEY'RE OFF!

"This is it," said Maverick, giving himself
a pep talk. "The big one. Time to make it count.
When it really matters. Everything to play
for . . ."

Jimmy chewed on his fingernails. He looked
at the start line.

"Maverick looks like he's been in a fight with
a garbage truck," he heard Horace shouting to
Chip.

"It's a race, not a beauty contest," Chip
yelled back.

Leadpipe's airship hovered in the blue sky
above them. As they watched, Lord Leadpipe's

jolly face appeared on a giant screen, peering down at the contestants through his monocle.

"Ladies and gentlemen," he said, his big red face beaming and his voice ringing around the Canyon, "it gives me great pleasure to welcome you all to the first-ever Robot Races for under-sixteens. Today's race will see our drivers taking on the challenges of the incredible Grand Canyon and battling for the lead in the Robot Races Championship."

"Look at them all," said Jimmy sadly as Lord Leadpipe continued to warm up the crowd. "Dug and Monster and Lightning. They all look so good."

"Yeah. Let's just give up and go home," said Maverick.

"What?" Jimmy spluttered. "But it's the Robot Races! We can't quit now! I've wanted to do this my whole life!" He trailed off as he realized what Maverick was trying to do.

"Exactly. Now, come on, Jimmy!" Maverick yelled. "We're in this race, and we'll show those fancy, shiny robots how it's done."

"You're right." Jimmy gripped the steering wheel. "Let's show them what we can do."

Jimmy jumped as Grandpa's voice crackled out of a little radio on Maverick's dashboard.

"Everything okay, Jimmy?"

"Everything's fine, Grandpa," Jimmy said nervously.

"Everything's just peachy," said Maverick. "A-okay. Ticketyboo. Hunky dory. Couldn't be better. We are so ready! So let's get this show on the road."

"ON YOUR MARKS . . .!" yelled Lord Leadpipe suddenly.

Jimmy looked for the ignition button. Then looked again. A cold shudder ran through him, and he desperately started searching the panel in front of him.

"It's gone!" he cried.

"What's gone?" said Grandpa and Maverick together.

"The big red ignition button. The thing that makes us go! Where is it?" Jimmy said, starting to sweat.

"GET SET!" Lord Leadpipe's voice echoed around the racetrack. The other racers' engines filled the air with a rumbling roar.

"Oh," said Grandpa, as though he had just remembered something. "I meant to tell you. I did move some of the gadgets around. One or two last-minute adjustments."

"I've got it!" shrieked Jimmy, pressing a red button on Maverick's ceiling.

"GO!" Leadpipe bellowed.

With a click and a rush of air, a hatch in Maverick's roof flew open. An enormous magnet on a chain shot up to the sky. It quickly came clattering down, narrowly missing an elderly spectator and his dog.

Zoom, Dug, Monster, Lightning, and Maximus all roared into the distance, covering Maverick in a cloud of dust.

"I think that's the wrong button," Grandpa said helpfully.

"What do I do? What do I do?" said Jimmy.

"Don't panic!" Maverick said. "I'm making the ignition button flash."

Jimmy stared around frantically, and finally found the big red button at the side of the steering wheel.

"Okay," he said firmly. He pressed the flashing red button, and Maverick's engine roared into life.

"A little revving for show," said Maverick, gunning his engine then reeling in the magnet as fast as he could, "and here we go! We're off!"

Jimmy jammed his foot down on the accelerator. They burst out onto the winding track on a ridge high inside the Grand Canyon.

"Don't look down, Jimmy," Maverick warned.

"Why not?" answered Jimmy, looking down. He immediately regretted it. He saw a sheer drop to the thin silver line of the river about a mile below.

His heart climbed into his throat. He gripped the steering wheel like he was hanging on for his life. Then he focused on the road ahead, steering steadily between the cliff face to their left and the drop to their right, aiming for the dust cloud thrown up by the racers ahead.

"We've got to catch them," he said through gritted teeth. "But I can't even see them."

"I can help with that," Maverick said. "Push the windshield zoom." A little purple button popped up on the windshield and started to flash. Jimmy pressed it. A corner of the windshield magnified the glass. It felt like Jimmy was looking through a pair of binoculars.

In the distance, Horace and Zoom were trying to edge past Monster's huge wheels. The road wasn't wide enough for them both. As Jimmy watched, Zoom did a daring overtake on the winding lane and edged past Missy and Monster. Jimmy had to admit that Horace and Zoom made a pretty good team.

"Come on, Maverick, we can't lose them!" he said.

"We're gaining on them," Maverick replied as they shot past a blur of cliff face and sand. "If we can keep this speed up, we'll catch them in . . ." He paused for less than a second to calculate. ". . . just under three minutes and seven seconds."

"Let's go, then!" cried Jimmy. He was still sweating. His heart was beating a million times a second. That feeling of excitement and concentration was taking over. He had a job to do, and that was to get Maverick to the finish line as quickly as possible.

"Curve in the road ahead," warned Maverick.

Jimmy remembered a similar winding cliff-top track in one of the races he'd watched last year. Big Al and Crusher had taken it too fast and crashed. He eased off the pedal slightly. He took the corner smoothly before hitting the accelerator again.

"Nice driving," said Maverick. They rounded the corner. Then Maverick sped up as they hit a straight section of track. They could see the other racers ahead in a distant cloud of dust. Jimmy scanned the buttons in front of him for something that could help.

"Hit the rocket-boosters, Jimmy!" cried Maverick.

"Maybe we should save them," Jimmy replied. "We might need a boost later on."

Then he noticed something on the zoom screen. Far ahead, the other racers were being called into a pit stop by their teams.

Chip and Dug got there first, skidding toward the waiting mechanics who leaped on the racer and went to work. Kako and Lightning were right behind them. Maximus and Zoom bashed into each other, sparks flying, as they crashed into their spaces. In front of Maverick, Missy and Monster were slowing down for a stop too.

In the last space there was a little figure waving. He had wild hair that was blowing all over the place. It was Grandpa.

"First pit stop coming up," crackled Grandpa's voice over the intercom. "Get ready to pull in, Jimmy."

"This is our chance!" Jimmy gasped. "Maverick, do we really need to stop?"

"Well . . ." said Maverick, doing a quick check of his functions. "The front tire is a little worn. The engine might need a little tune-up and a little oil. I need water. And fuel."

"Grandpa?" said Jimmy into the intercom. "Can Maverick take water from his water cannon and fuel from the rocket-boosters?"

"I don't know, Jimmy. I've never tried it," Grandpa's voice crackled over the intercom.

"Already done it," said Maverick.

"Awesome!" cried Jimmy. "We're going on!"

Grandpa stood open-mouthed as they sailed past him, past all the other racers, and went into the lead. In his mirror, Jimmy could see the small white-haired figure, bouncing up and down and punching the air.

Grandpa's voice came over the intercom. "Go, Jimmy, go!"

Jimmy cheered and then panicked. He'd never seen a robot racer miss a pit stop before. What if it was the wrong thing to do?

"How far is it to the next pit stop?" he asked anxiously.

"Forty-two miles," said Maverick.

"Will we make it all right?"

"Make it?" cried Maverick. "Of course we'll make it! There are parts of me that spent twenty years on the taxi circuit! Those other racers might need their fancy paint work touched up and their wheels massaged, but with enough water and fuel we can keep going forever!"

Jimmy grinned as Maverick switched on the zoom screen to show the view behind them. He was sure the other racers would catch up soon, but for the moment, they were actually winning!

CHAPTER 11
DIRTY TRICKS

The road started to climb. Maverick went faster. They snaked left, then right, then left again. Jimmy was growing in confidence all the time. The road began to narrow until the ledge they were driving on was only slightly wider than Maverick. Jimmy glanced over at the sheer drop on their right. His stomach did a couple of nervous somersaults.

"No one can overtake us here!" shouted Maverick, just as the other robot racers appeared in their mirrors. They were gaining fast.

"Whoa!" yelled Jimmy as they rounded a curve and Maverick's back end swung out over the edge of the cliff. "Let's keep all four wheels on the road, Maverick."

As the robot racer found his grip again, Jimmy heard a faint cheer from the crowd watching from the canyon's edge. Jimmy guided Maverick into another sharp corner.

"Look out!" cried Jimmy, slamming on the brakes. The road ahead was completely blocked by a huge rock slide, but Maverick was still skidding toward the mountain of rocks and boulders. Jimmy stiffened, bracing himself for the impact.

"Don't worry. I've got this all under control," said Maverick calmly. He hit the retro-rockets, which fired instantly, bringing them to a stop just in front of the rock slide.

As Jimmy peered through the windshield, he could see Maverick's front tires smoking. A cloud of dust had flown up around them. Next to them, the cliff dropped down to the river below, a tumbling slope of red rocks and dust.

"I didn't see this from the airship," Jimmy complained.

"It wasn't there before," Maverick confirmed. "I think this is the first challenge of the race. You know there are obstacles on each track."

Jimmy glanced nervously at the vertical rock face on his left, at the sheer drop down into the canyon on his right, and at the rock pile ahead. "Can we get over it?" Jimmy thought out loud. "Or through it? Or under it?"

"The others are gaining on us," said Maverick. "Whatever we do, we need to do it quickly!"

"Okay," said Jimmy. "How do we get over it?"

"We . . ." Maverick paused and thought, his computer whirring. "We fire the pogo-thruster. The button's flashing blue now."

"The pogo-thruster?" repeated Jimmy nervously. "What does it do?"

"Rockets us into the sky," said Maverick. "We'll land on the other side of the rock slide."

"But it's a windy day. What if we don't land on the other side?" asked Jimmy. "What if it rockets us into the sky and we're blown down into the Canyon?"

"Good point," said Maverick.

"Can we get around it?" asked Jimmy.

"There's a small ledge at the edge of the rock slide," said Maverick. "We reverse, accelerate, go up on two wheels, and —"

"And crash over the edge," finished Jimmy. "Or crash into the rock slide. Do you have any suggestions that don't involve us crashing?"

Maverick thought for a moment. "No," he said.

"Let's back up and get a good look at it," said Jimmy.

Maverick quickly reversed. But as he did, Lightning appeared from nowhere and zipped around him, heading straight for the rock slide. At the last moment, steel ropes and grappling hooks flew from Lightning's front shield, grabbing hold of the rock face and pulling Princess Kako and her robobike up and over the mound of fallen rocks.

"We need to do something. Here comes Monster!" said Jimmy, looking in the rearview display screen. But it was too late.

Missy and her enormous monster truck racer swerved around them. The truck's front grille dropped down, and out came a drill, spinning into a blur. Dust and rocks and splinters flew up as the drill burrowed into the ground. Monster disappeared down the tunnel she had dug beneath the rock slide.

"Now's our chance," cried Jimmy, stamping on the accelerator. "Let's follow them!"

Maverick's engine roared, and they flew backward.

"Oops," said Maverick. "Still in reverse!"

Jimmy flicked the gear paddle into first gear, but before he could power forward, Sammy and his hoverbot, Maximus, had barged in front of them and skimmed into the darkness of the tunnel.

"Come on!" cried Jimmy as Zoom, then Dug, hurtled past and headed for the opening.

"Fire the jet-thrusters and let's get going!" yelled Maverick.

Jimmy was reaching for the flashing green button when they heard a screech of tires at the entrance to the tunnel. Zoom had stopped. Jimmy could see Horace pressing all sorts of buttons on the roof of the sports car.

"What's he doing?" Jimmy cried. "He's blocking the way!"

"Even Horace Pelly can't be that stupid," said Maverick. "He won't win sitting there!"

"And neither will we," groaned Jimmy. "Horace is even worse than he used to be. He will do anything to win!"

A nasty grin had spread across Horace's face. "Dig your way out of this one, Chippy," he yelled over the roar of his engine.

Two pipes shot out from beneath Zoom's bumper. One sprayed water all over the racetrack. The other sent clouds of white smoke billowing across it.

When it cleared, the water had frozen and turned the track into a dangerous ice rink!

Dug was racing toward the tunnel at top speed. He hit the ice and had no hope of staying under control. Dug tried desperately to grip the path, but he couldn't.

Dug's pincer arm flailed. He grabbed at the ice, helplessly trying to steady himself as he skidded toward the cliff edge.

Jimmy watched Chip's mouth open in a silent, terrified scream as he plunged backward and disappeared over the side of the cliff.

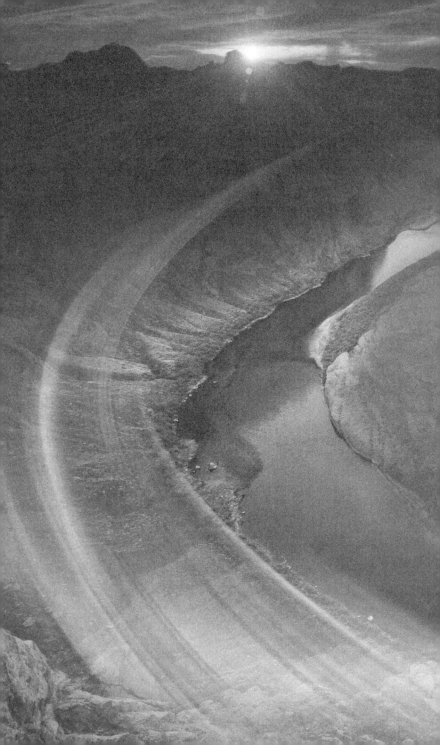

CHAPTER 12
OVER THE EDGE

Jimmy sat frozen for a moment. He sat just long enough to see Horace and Zoom shooting off through the tunnel. Then he jumped out of Maverick and inched to the cliff edge. All Jimmy could think about was what he would see when he looked over the edge.

Hardly daring to open his eyes, Jimmy looked down. The floor of the Canyon was about a mile below them. Jimmy screwed up his eyes in the blazing heat of the sun, but all he could see was dust and sand and rocks. There was no sign of Dug or Chip.

"Help!" cried a voice. It sounded like Chip.

"Did you hear that?" asked Maverick.

"I heard it!" said Jimmy. "Chip!" he shouted down. "It's Jimmy. Are you all right? Where are you?"

"Down here!" said the voice.

Jimmy moved along the cliff, trying to edge closer to where the sound was coming from. When he found the spot, he carefully stretched a little further out over the Canyon. He looked straight down and saw Dug!

Jimmy cheered. There, resting about twenty yards directly below them, was the huge yellow racer. Dug appeared to be hanging in midair. Chip was poking his head out of the window, looking up at Jimmy and waving.

"How are they just floating there?" Jimmy asked Maverick.

"It's an invisible force field," said Maverick to Jimmy. "Lord Leadpipe must have had them installed for the race for safety."

"Thank goodness," Jimmy said. "Hold on, Chip."

He racked his brain for a way to help them up. None of the safetybots were hovering overhead. There was no sign of anyone who could help rescue Dug and Chip. It was up to Jimmy. He ran over to Maverick and got in.

"What are we doing?" asked Maverick. "Let's fire up the engines and catch those other losers!"

"We're not going anywhere," said Jimmy.

"What?" said Maverick.

"We've got to help Chip and Dug," said Jimmy. "We're their only hope!" He scanned the rows of buttons on his control panel, looking for something he could use to help Chip.

"Yes!" cried Jimmy excitedly, remembering the huge magnet flying out of Maverick's roof at the start of the race. "Maverick, I'm firing the Magnetic SuperPull over the cliff edge. Okay?"

"I can do better than that," replied Maverick. "Press the green button. It's flashing now."

"What is it?" asked Jimmy, punching the button.

"The Magnetic SuperPull Crane-o-matic," replied Maverick proudly. And before Jimmy could ask any more questions, he felt four heavy thuds. Thick legs extended under Maverick.

Jimmy opened his window and stuck his head out to get a better view. A hatch opened on Maverick's roof. An enormous crane arm rose into the air. The Magnetic SuperPull fired out of the roof and flew down into the Canyon.

"Just like fishing," Maverick said. "Not that I've ever been fishing before."

Jimmy got out of Maverick and hurried over to the cliff edge. The huge magnet swung on its chain, but it was too short.

"It's not long enough!" called Chip.

Oh, no, thought Jimmy. *There's no way of getting closer to them.*

Then suddenly he had an idea.

"Chip, you're going to have to reach up as far as you can. If you can get Dug's lifting arm close enough, the magnet will do the rest."

Everything seemed to be in slow motion. For a split second, it looked as if they were still too far away. The magnet swayed from side to side as Dug's long arm stretched to reach it.

Come on, come on, Jimmy thought.

Then suddenly there was a loud thunk that echoed around the Canyon.

"Yes! Reel them in, Maverick!" called Jimmy.

Maverick braced himself on his four stabilizing legs, tightened the chain, and began to heave.

Slowly, Maverick pulled Dug up. The digger swayed in the wind as it was hauled up. Clouds of black smoke poured from Maverick's exhaust. His engines were firing on full throttle to make enough power for the huge magnet.

"Yee-haa!" yelled Chip, punching the air in celebration. They slowly rose from the Canyon. Dug rose level with the racetrack, and Maverick swung the Crane-o-matic's huge arm around. He gently lowered Dug to the ground.

"That's some gadget!" called Chip, jumping down from his cab. "Thanks, guys. I thought it was over when we went flyin' over the edge." His face suddenly darkened. "I can't wait to get Dug's claws on Horace and his robot. What a jerk!"

"No problem," said Maverick. "Now does anyone think we should get going?"

"The race!" cried Jimmy and Chip together.

Chip jumped into Dug, and Jimmy jumped into Maverick. Side by side, they fired up their engines.

"After you!" called Chip. "It's the least I can do!"

Jimmy nodded his thanks, and Maverick shot through the gap in the rock slide with Dug following close behind. They flew out the other side of the tunnel to the deafening roar of hundreds of fans cheering, the noise spurring the two racers on to even greater speeds. It was definitely inspiring.

"Hello? Hello?" crackled a familiar voice on Maverick's intercom.

"Grandpa!" said Jimmy.

"Where are you?" said Grandpa. He sounded worried. "Four of the other competitors have made their second pit stop already."

"We had a little problem," said Jimmy. "It's all figured out now."

"I don't know what you've been doing to him," said Grandpa, "but it looks like Maverick's blown seven or eight fuses. Your rocket fuel's nearly on zero. That wipes out the rocket-boosters, and you're going to need them. Pit stop in two miles. You'd better pull in this time."

"Another holdup?" grumbled Maverick. "Rock falls, rescue missions, pit stops . . . why don't we stop for a cup of tea and a slice of cake as well?"

"Come on, Maverick," said Jimmy. "Grandpa needs to check you over. We'll never win if you're not in top condition. There it is!"

Maverick slowed and pulled into position at the pit stop, just seconds ahead of Chip and Dug.

Grandpa stuck his head in the window, filling the cab with his huge white hair. "You're doing amazing, my boy." He grinned. "I'll get under the hood and have a quick tune-up. Then you can get on your way."

Jimmy sat patiently while Grandpa ran a computer check on Maverick's functions and made some small adjustments. Grandpa danced around the taxi like a man half his age, inserting a new microchip here and replacing a blown fuse there.

After just a few moments he shouted, "All clear! Off you go, my boy."

"Right," said Jimmy as Maverick fired up his engines. "Time for some speed, Maverick. I'm putting my foot down."

"About time!" exclaimed Maverick, his tires squealing. "Full speed ahead!"

CHAPTER 13
BACK IN THE RACE

Jimmy and Maverick shot out of the pit lane in a cloud of dust. Chip's mechanics climbed all over Dug, tightening bolts and hammering out dents after the bashing he had taken. Monster, Zoom, Maximus, and Lightning were nowhere to be seen.

"We've got some catching up to do, Maverick," said Jimmy.

"Rocket-boosters?" suggested Maverick.

"Not yet. There's a long way to go. We might need them for a fast finish."

They sped on for the next few miles without any incidents. Maverick and Jimmy stayed quiet, focusing on the track in front of them. But as they rounded a corner and began to climb a long, steep hill, they got their first glimpse of another team. Just ahead of them on the hill were Missy and Monster.

"Why are they going so slow?" asked Jimmy.

"Too heavy to get up the hills," said Maverick.

Maverick darted to the right of Monster. Monster swerved and blocked him. Maverick darted to the left. Monster blocked him again.

"And too wide and sneaky for us to get past," muttered Maverick.

"What do we do?" asked Jimmy.

"I've got it!" said Maverick. "I know a way to get past Missy."

"Just tell me what to do," said Jimmy.

"Drop back. We need a little space between us and Monster," said Maverick.

Jimmy eased off the accelerator. The gap between Maverick and Monster widened.

"Perfect," said Maverick. "Now maintain that speed and, when I say so, press the flashing orange button on the top right of the control panel."

"Okay," said Jimmy.

"Now!" said Maverick.

Jimmy pressed the orange button. With a whoosh and a flash of black, a rocket shot out from under Maverick. It soared high into the air, and then fell downward sharply. As it plummeted back toward earth, it unfolded into a steep ramp. It hit the ground just behind Monster.

With a whoop of excitement, Jimmy hit the accelerator pedal to the floor. He gripped the steering wheel for dear life. They hit the ramp at top speed and flew high over the monster truck.

In a strange, still moment of silence, Jimmy could see nothing through Maverick's windshield but blue sky. His stomach seemed to be in his throat. He didn't dare breathe.

Then Maverick began to tip forward. He landed with a thump, kicking up a mountain of dust behind them.

"Amazing!" screamed Jimmy. "Genius!"

"Thank you," said Maverick calmly. "I've been looking forward to using that."

"Shoot!" they heard Missy shout as they roared away. "Monster, you great big dingo! Why do you have to be such a lardy boot?"

Leaving the red-haired girl and her racer far behind, Maverick and Jimmy flew over the top of the hill.

"Now let's find the others and get past them," Jimmy said. He hit the windshield zoom-in button. It showed Horace Pelly and Zoom in the lead. Sammy and Maximus were just behind them. Princess Kako and Lightning brought up the rear of the group.

"I'm at top speed," said Maverick, soaring around a curve on two wheels. "We'll catch them in the next five minutes."

"Excellent," said Jimmy.

Zoom was now in the lead. Maximus and Lightning were right behind him, dodging left and right. They were looking for space to take the lead. The road narrowed. The cliff crumbled as Maximus slid dangerously close to the edge.

All three robot racers were now bumping and hitting each other, swerving wildly and taking risks to get the upper hand.

Maximus made another dart toward the left. Before he could drag himself alongside Zoom, there was a deafening bang. Suddenly the giant hovercraft seemed to hit an invisible wall. It flew high into the air, spinning back over the roof of Maverick.

"What the . . ." Jimmy whispered.

"He's going over the edge!" Maverick said.

But Maverick was wrong. Maximus was swept into a vicious-looking clump of cacti. As Jimmy sped past he heard a long, loud ripping sound. The cacti tore a deep hole into the bottom of the racer's air cushion. The gas inside came whooshing out, making a low hissing noise.

Sammy climbed out awkwardly, trying to avoid the nasty spikes on the nearest cactus. When he saw the tear in the side of his racer, he scowled and stamped his foot. There was no way he could finish today.

Sammy and Maximus were out of the race.

"Wow!" breathed Jimmy, forcing his eyes back onto the road in time to see something blue glowing above Zoom's rear bumper.

"What's that?" he shouted.

"It looks like Zoom's using some kind of force field," replied Maverick. "It burns out electrical circuits on anything that comes near it. That's what threw Maximus off the track. The moment anyone tries to overtake Zoom, he'll fry their circuits!"

CHAPTER 14
THE FINISH LINE

Maverick and Lightning raced side by side, both keeping a safe distance from Zoom and his deadly force field.

"There's no way we can win if we're stuck behind Zoom," said Jimmy impatiently. "We've got to do something."

"The pogo-thruster!" cried Maverick. "We can be up and over him before you can say —"

"No," said Jimmy. "We'll jump straight off the cliff. I've got another plan. You get as close as you dare. Pull to the right like you're going to overtake. He'll swerve right to block us. So we dart left. The track's wider here. If we can get past Zoom on the inside fast enough, we might get through without getting fried."

"That sounds dangerous," said Maverick. "I like it!"

As they moved toward Zoom, all Jimmy could focus on was the blue light. It buzzed and growled. He could feel the air crackling with electricity as the force field reached full charge again.

"Here we go," said Maverick, his voice shaking with the speed.

"Go, Maverick, go!" Jimmy cried, hitting the accelerator as hard as he could. He swerved one way first. Then he darted to the other, just as they'd planned. The robot's engine roared. They began to pull alongside Zoom.

"Yes. We're doing it!" Jimmy yelled. "We're going to make it!"

The air suddenly fizzed. A wave of hot energy rolled over Maverick as Horace fired the force field.

"If I can just go —" stuttered Maverick. "I think —" he went on, "engine what magnet . . ."

"Maverick?" Jimmy cried in alarm. "What's wrong?"

A large orange triangle started flashing and blinking on Maverick's control panel.

"Error. Error. Error . . ." said Maverick repeatedly, his voice fading into silence. They were slowing down, dropping back from Zoom, now level with Lightning.

"Ha, ha! You're finished now, Roberts," Jimmy heard Horace shout over the noise of the racers. "Your old rust bucket never stood a chance against Zoom."

But Jimmy didn't care about Horace Pelly at that moment. He was too worried about his friend.

"Maverick?" he said urgently. "Maverick? Talk to me."

He stomped on the accelerator. Nothing happened. The roar of Maverick's engines fell to a sickly whir. Then nothing. Complete silence.

Lightning was ahead of them, and Zoom was ahead of Lightning. Soon Maverick would come to a stop.

Jimmy started frantically pushing buttons but nothing happened. "Don't give up, Maverick. We're so close to the finish."

Suddenly there was a loud beep. Every light and button on Maverick's huge control panel started flashing — randomly at first, and then in order.

At the same time, Zoom began to lose speed. The blue light dimmed. The grinding noise faded. Jimmy could feel cold, fresh air on his face once again as Maverick's cooling systems returned.

The orange triangle on the control panel stopped flashing. The hum of Maverick's power returned, progressing from a whir, to a purr, to a growl, to a roar.

"Ha!" shouted Maverick. "That force field uses thousands of volts a second. Using it twice in a row has sapped Zoom's power. Let's go!"

"Are you feeling okay?" asked Jimmy.

"Much better," said Maverick. "There's nothing like a total reboot and self-repair to set you up for the day." He shot back up to full speed, and within seconds he had drawn level with Zoom.

From the corner of one eye, Jimmy caught a glimpse of Horace shouting and pounding at Zoom's controls with his fists. He looked angrier than usual.

"Come on, you hunk of junk," he was shouting. "I won't be beaten by that terrible excuse for a robot racer."

Maverick edged ahead, but Zoom was quickly getting back to full power. As the road widened and the finish line got closer, Maverick, Lightning, and Zoom were neck and neck.

Jimmy glanced across at Princess Kako in her silver leather suit and helmet, her face hidden behind a black visor. Then he fixed his eyes back on the road, concentrating on every bend, every rock, every inch of the racetrack.

Without warning, a thundering blaze of flame exploded from Lightning's exhaust. Princess Kako shot ahead at an incredible speed.

"Time for the rocket-boosters, Jimmy!" said Maverick. "The red button's flashing."

"Not yet, Maverick," said Jimmy, his voice calm and steady as Lightning sailed into the distance. "We only have ten seconds of rocket fuel left in the tank. We've only got one chance. We've got to get it right."

He glanced across at Zoom. For a moment, his eyes met Horace's. Jimmy saw the other boy's gritted teeth, his face covered with anger.

Not looking so smug now, is he? Jimmy thought.

"Come on! We need rocket-boosters now!" Maverick yelled again.

"Not yet, Maverick!" shouted back Jimmy above the roar of the engine.

"But look!" shouted Maverick. "The finish line!"

Ahead, a huge crowd had gathered at the finish line, and the black-and-white checkered flags were flapping in the wind. Jimmy rested his finger on the flashing red rocket-booster button.

"The finish is straight ahead," warned Maverick, his voice getting more urgent. Zoom and Maverick hurtled toward it, getting every last ounce of speed out of their engines.

Jimmy wiped his sweaty hand on his jeans. He rested his finger on the flashing button once more. Princess Kako and Lightning were getting further away and were nearly across the finish line.

We can't catch Princess Kako, Jimmy said to himself. *But there's no way I'm letting a spoiled brat like Horace Pelly beat me.*

He locked eyes with Horace as the two racers touched wheels. As the princess crossed the line, punching a fist into the air and saluting the screaming crowd, Jimmy took a deep breath and pressed the flashing button!

The world blurred for a second as the rocket-boosters fired up. Jimmy was forced back into his seat as Maverick went from fast to super-fast in a single second.

"Nooooooo!" shrieked Horace as Jimmy and Maverick hit the finish line, just one second in front of Zoom.

The crowd roared. The checkered flag waved. What a finish! As Maverick fired his retro-rockets to slow them to a stop, Jimmy looked out of the window at thousands of smiling faces in the stands.

He stuck his head out of Maverick's window, raised his hands in the air to salute the fans and shouted, "Yeeeeesss!"

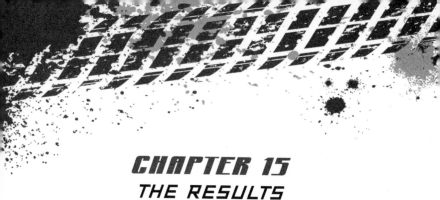

CHAPTER 15
THE RESULTS

"We did it, Maverick!" Jimmy whooped in delight.

"Well done, Jimmy," said Maverick.

"Me?" said Jimmy, grinning broadly. "Well done, Maverick, I think you mean!"

"We were a pretty good team, weren't we?" the robot replied.

"I didn't think we'd finish the race, let alone come in second!" Jimmy laughed. "And we beat Horace Pelly!"

Jimmy watched in disbelief as the other racers crossed the line.

"Come on," said Maverick, firing up his engines again, "let's look at the results board." They headed for the main grandstand, where a huge hovering display board was just about to show the final results.

"What are we waiting for?" Jimmy wondered aloud, climbing out of Maverick. "Everyone knows Princess Kako came first and we came second."

The display boards flashed, numbers whirring. High above them sailed Lord Leadpipe's airship, his grinning face projected on its side once more.

"Ladies and gentlemen," boomed Lord Leadpipe's voice from the loudspeakers on the massive airship, "the results of this thrilling first leg of the Robot Races Championship are as follows . . ."

"In first place, with ten points," boomed Lord Leadpipe, "Princess Kako and Lightning."

"In second place, with eight points," said Lord Leadpipe, "Jimmy Roberts and Maverick!"

Jimmy felt his heart swell in his chest until he thought it would explode.

"In third place," said Lord Leadpipe, "Horace Pelly and Zoom. But," continued Lord Leadpipe, "Horace Pelly will have two points deducted following the use of unauthorized gadgetry and suspicious conduct."

"What!" screeched Horace Pelly. "Unauthorized? Suspicious? Is he calling me a cheater? Dad!" he shrieked, stamping his foot. "Dad! Get over here! And bring those NASA idiots with you!"

"So Horace Pelly and Zoom have four points," continued Lord Leadpipe. "They tied for third place with Chip Travers and Dug. Missy McGovern and Monster have two points. Samir Bahur and Maximus did not complete the course."

Jimmy and Maverick were swamped by reporters asking them all kinds of questions.

"How did you feel, knowing everyone thought you would come in last?"

"How do you feel about coming in second?"

"What are your chances in the next race?"

"Who built your racer?"

Jimmy stood with his mouth open and only one thought in his head: *find Grandpa.*

"I'll answer that question," came Maverick's voice from behind Jimmy. "At first, we played it cool. Keeping our heads down. Not wanting to take the lead, but —"

Jimmy pushed his way through the crowd, leaving Maverick to enjoy his moment in the spotlight. He was looking for a glimpse of Grandpa's wild white hair. And there it was, bobbing its way toward him. He had his arms outstretched, with a huge smile on his face. Jimmy leaped into Grandpa's arms.

"Well done, my boy," Grandpa finally said. "Well done!"

"Thanks for your help out there," said Chip, pushing through the crowd and shaking Jimmy by the hand until his arm ached. "I'd still be there now if you hadn't come along and saved me."

"No problem," said Jimmy.

"Congratulations, Jimmy," said a familiar voice behind him.

Jimmy turned slowly to meet the twinkling eyes and rosy red cheeks of Lord Leadpipe. "You and Maverick drove a marvelous race. Beautifully done. That's one of the finest performances I think I've seen in all my years. And certainly one of the closest finishes."

His smile broadened. "Why don't you introduce me to the rest of your team? Is this your mechanic over here?" Lord Leadpipe turned to Grandpa. "Good lord," he said. "You're . . . I mean, it's —"

"Wilfred Roberts," finished Grandpa coldly. "Hello, Ludwick. It's been a long time."

"It's so nice to see you after all these years," Lord Leadpipe said, a smile spreading across his face. "But what are you doing here?"

"Jimmy's my grandson," explained Grandpa, his voice growing colder. "And I built his racer, Maverick. My robot might not be as flashy and shiny as some of yours, but I've still got a few robo-tricks up my sleeves."

"Well," said Lord Leadpipe, looking flustered, "it's lovely to see you again."

"Is it?" snapped Grandpa. "I wish I could say the same."

"Well," Lord Leadpipe went on, trying to fix a smile on his face as a swarm of newspaper reporters and photographers surrounded them, "you've got a grandson to be proud of. I noticed him stopping to help one of the other competitors who was in trouble. Not every driver would do such a thing. Either of you," said Lord Leadpipe turning to Jimmy and Chip, "could have won that race, you know."

Jimmy and Chip looked at each other and smiled.

"And who knows," added Lord Leadpipe, "one of you may win the next leg of the Robot Races Championship. Speaking of which, I have an announcement to make."

Lord Leadpipe waved a hand in the air. Joshua Johnson, the Robot Coordinator with the enormous eyebrows, came running over with a microphone. He still had cotton stuffed in his ears.

"Ladies and gentlemen," Lord Leadpipe said into the microphone, his voice ringing out around the Grand Canyon. "I am delighted to announce that the next stage of the Robot Races Championship will take place in just one month's time. I can't reveal where just yet, but rest assured it will be another action-packed, adrenaline-fueled, no-holds-barred fight to the checkered flag! We look forward to seeing you all there! And remember, keep racing!"

Jimmy and Grandpa looked at Maverick, and then at each other, their eyes twinkling with excitement.

"A month?" said Maverick, revving his engines. "Grandpa, get your tools. We've got work to do! Today's race might be finished, but the championship's only just begun!"

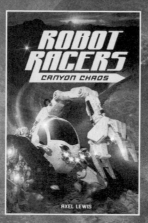

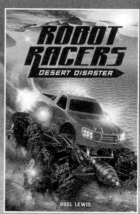